'The eighth and penultimate book in the *Wolf Brother* series and a compelling standalone, *Skin Taker*, is a story of survival, despite the capricious nature and fragility of Stone Age life.'

Armadillo

'Fascinating insights into the characters' understanding of the world they live in. The story is one of adventure, mystery and suspense…'

Books for Topics

'This book is a novel to be cherished, treasured and loved by every young generation to come.'

LoveReading4Kids

'*Skin Taker* is another masterpiece: powerful, riveting and breathtaking.'

Toppsta

Viper's Daughter

This book is due for return on or before the last date shown below. It may be renewed by telephone, personal application, fax or post, quoting this date, author, title and the book number.

Skin Taker

'… can easily be read as a standalone novel, so skilful is the storytelling… Paver powerfully presents a world view that's magical but never primitive…'

Financial Times

'[*Skin Taker*] with its vivid imagery, skilful world-building and tense storyline is a compelling read.'

Just Imagine

'… incredible language and spectacular world-building… An outstanding fantasy adventure that is complex, exciting and absolutely unputdownable.'

BookTrust

'Top-class storytelling in the eighth book in the stormingly good *Wolf Brother* series.'

Fiona Noble, *The Bookseller*

'Another outstanding story, *Skin Taker*, like its fellows, deserves more than one reading to truly appreciate the detail and care with which it has been written. I cannot wait for the final instalment.'

ReadingZone

WOLF BANE

Also by Michelle Paver in this series

For older readers

WOLF BANE

MICHELLE PAVER

ZEPHYR

an imprint of Head of Zeus

First published in the UK in 2022 by Zephyr, an imprint of Head of Zeus Ltd
This Zephyr paperback edition first published in the UK in 2022 by Head of Zeus Ltd,
part of Bloomsbury Publishing Plc

9 7 5 3 1 2 4 6 8

A catalogue record for this book is available
from the British Library.

ISBN (PB): 9781789542455
ISBN (E): 9781789542462

Typeset by Ed Pickford

Printed and bound in Great Britain
by CPI Group (UK) Ltd, Croydon CR0 4YY

Head of Zeus Ltd
5–8 Hardwick Street
London EC1R 4RG

WWW.HEADOFZEUS.COM

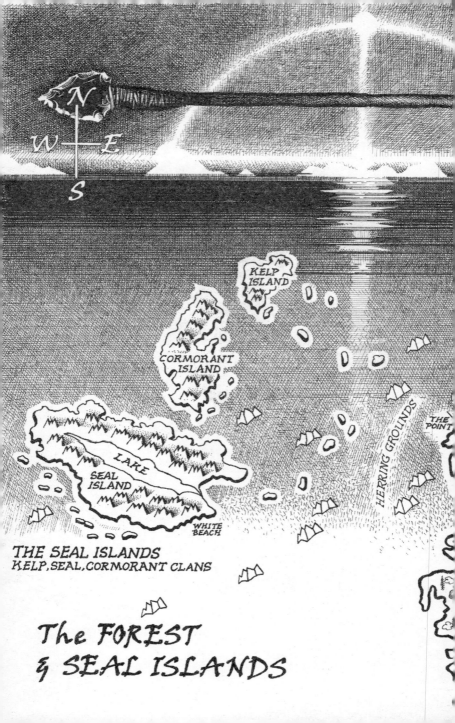

TO THE
FAR NORTH
WHITE FOX, NARWAL, PTARMIGAN
WALRUS CLANS

RIVER BLACKTHORN

ICE RIVER

THE HIGH
MOUNTAINS

SWAN, ROWAN, MOUNTAIN HARE CLANS

WOLF CLAN

GREEN RIVER

ICE RIVER

WHITEWATER

TWIN RIVERS

CLAN RIDGE

RIVER AXEHANDLE

HOGBACK

LAKE AXEHEAD
OTTER CLAN

CROWWATER

SPARE DEN

RAVEN CLAN

DEN

WIDEWATER

THUNDER FALLS

BURNT LANDS

RIVER CUTSTONE

THE DEEP FOREST

ELK RIVER

THE NECK

BLACKWATER

RAVEN BONE-GROUND

THE SHIELD

SACRED GROVE

THE OPEN FOREST

RIDGE

WINDRIVER

WILLOW CLAN

RUSHWATER

HILLS

AUROCH, FOREST HORSE, RED DEER CLANS

TUMBLEROCK

RIVER HORSELEAP

× AUROCH ROCK

FASTWATER

REDWATER

× FA KILLED

FELLS

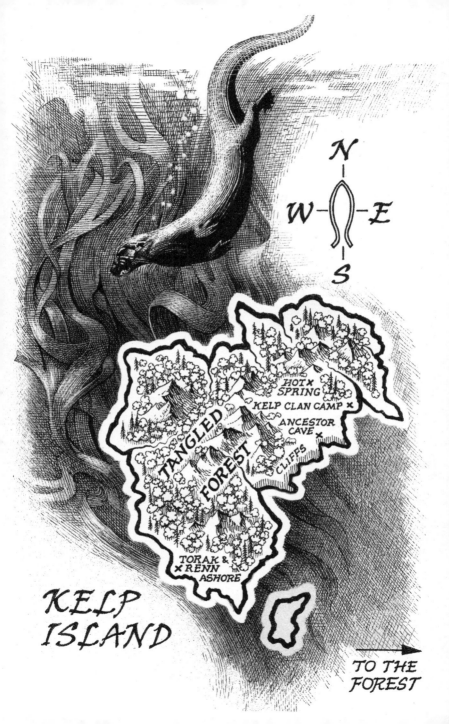

ONE

The wolves have no idea that the Demon is watching. No idea that their shiny little lives could be snuffed out in a heartbeat.

Since dawn the Demon has been observing them from the ridge. Through the snowbound pines it makes out the red boulders where the she-wolf is digging her den. She's inside. Two wolves are padding about among the rocks. They seem to be guarding her, but they're bored and eager to play. One snaps an icicle off a boulder and bounds away, the other gives chase.

Now the she-wolf is backing out of the den. Her black pelt is clotted with mud, her belly swollen with unborn cubs. Hungrily the Demon licks the tang of her spirit off the wind. It would be easy to kill her, a single arrow destroying many lives... But she is not the one the Demon wants. The Demon is after her mate.

There.

Far up-valley near the frozen river, two more wolves are weaving between the trees. The lesser one with the white throat doesn't count; the Demon's quarry is the great grey wolf. Such souls it has, unbearably bright! The Demon hates and hungers for those souls — it longs to devour them and gain their power. Then at last it will claw its way out of this mortal body and be free...

Prickling with desire, the Demon pushes off on its long bone skates and sweeps downhill. It finds a snowbound thicket within arrowshot and downwind of the den. The she-wolf has gone back inside. Her 'guardians' play on, oblivious.

The Demon takes an arrow from its quiver and sniffs the poison on its black flint head. It nocks the arrow to its bow.

Sooner or later, her mate will return. Yes.

The Demon settles to wait.

In the next valley to the south, Renn, studying the tracks Torak had found, caught a shiver of malice on the wind and lifted her head.

'What's wrong?' said Torak with his eyes on the snow.

'Not sure. Maybe just a trace of his presence.'

'But only a trace,' he said in disgust. 'If this *is* his trail it's two days old.'

In the distance Wolf howled. Torak cupped his hands to his mouth and howled back. An instant later they heard Wolf's deep-throated reply.

Renn threw Torak a questioning look. He shrugged. 'Whitethroat went after another beaver.'

'Are they allright?'

'Yes. Why?' He was walking slowly, his lean brown face remote as he scanned the snow for signs.

Renn didn't reply. Nine days into the Moon of Roaring Rivers, and by now every valley should be noisy with cracking, grinding ice – and yet the thaw hadn't come. Winter still held the Forest in its grip. Was this why she felt a creeping unease?

Rip flew onto an overhead branch, scattering her with snow. 'I wish you wouldn't do that,' Renn muttered, brushing off her reindeer-hide parka. The raven fluffed his chin-feathers and gave her a gurgling greeting, then flew off, scattering more snow.

It's probably just lack of sleep, Renn told herself. Yesterday while making arrowheads she'd nicked the ball of her thumb, and the cut was swollen and painful. Last night's storm hadn't helped either. It was well out to Sea, nowhere near their camp, but since the Thunderstar struck, the most distant growl of thunder was enough to jolt her awake in a cold sweat.

Three moons since the disaster, and although the Burnt Lands were further east, even here by the coast the Forest bore scars: earlier they'd passed a swathe of pines felled by an earthshake.

Torak was beckoning to her and she hurried towards him, her snowshoes whispering over drifts.

3

He'd found a bootprint, boldly stamped for all to see.

'It's him, isn't it?' she said.

He nodded. 'Left foot turns slightly inwards. And I found this snagged on a branch.' Between finger and thumb he held up three long strands of yellow hair.

'Naiginn,' Renn said between her teeth.

Torak made to cast away the hairs but she took them from him. 'I may have a use for them.'

'A finding charm?'

'Maybe.'

'What's that over there?' he said in an altered voice.

Ten paces off, a young birch tree was dying. Its white bark had been wantonly slashed, and whoever had attacked it had made sure it would die by slicing away the soft bast underneath.

'Only a demon kills without reason,' growled Torak.

Nearby in the snow they found the body of an otter. Naiginn had eaten its eyes, tongue and brain, and had left the rest to rot, violating the Pact which forbade wasting any part of a kill.

A muscle worked in Torak's jaw. 'Scrabble marks in the snow. As if – oh no, she can't have been alive when…'

Renn felt sick with revulsion – and *shame*. Naiginn was her half-brother, her bone kin: an ice demon trapped in the body of a young man.

She pictured his once-handsome face, one side now puckered and scorched. His ice-blue eyes with their lightless black pupils. No human feeling, no sense of right or wrong.

Dead meat only gives me the taste *of souls,* he'd told Torak once. *I need* living *flesh! Every frightened, fluttering spirit makes me stronger – it loosens my bonds!*

Slipping off her mittens, Renn wrapped Naiginn's coiled hairs in a scrap of bast from the murdered birch and stowed them in her medicine pouch. While Torak laid his palm on the tree-trunk and quietly asked the Forest to help its souls find a new home, she stroked the otter's rich fur and bade its spirit be at peace. But was that possible if Naiginn had eaten its souls?

'Can you sense him at all?' Torak asked in a low voice.

She shook her head. Pushing back the sleeves of her parka, she showed him the zigzag tattoos on her wrists. 'They're not itching. He's long gone.' She frowned. She had a nagging sense that there was something they were missing.

Torak seemed to think so too. 'The last we heard of him,' he said thoughtfully, 'was the start of the Moon of Green Snow. Since then we've found no trace – until now. What was he doing *here*?'

'What do you mean?'

'Well, this part of the Forest's hardly deserted. The Willow Clan's camped just round that spur. Sea-eagles in the next valley, near the mouth of the Elk River, Raven Clan upstream from them, then us and the wolves. And he knows we're after him, he knows the clans are on the lookout – so why is he blatantly *here*?'

'He's bad at hiding? He's from the Far North, doesn't know the Forest as we do.'

'But he knows enough to cover his tracks. Think about it, Renn. Three days ago he just *happened* to meet those Whale Clan fishermen out at the herring grounds – and "let slip" that he was heading here, to the Windriver?'

'He did give them a false name—'

'—but didn't bother hiding his clan-tattoos – or his scars! I think he *wanted* them to suspect that he wasn't who he said. He knew they'd tell Fin-Kedinn – and that we'd get to hear of it. And now he's left this trail for us to find... No, Renn, he's telling us, "Naiginn was here!"'

'Maybe he's daring us to come after him.'

'Mm.' Uneasily he fingered the green basalt axe jammed in his belt. 'He's after souls,' he mused. 'The brighter the better. So why bother with saplings?'

Suddenly Renn had a dreadful thought. Naiginn hungered for bright, strong souls – and one creature had the brightest of all. 'He's not after trees,' she said. 'This is a decoy.'

Torak's grey eyes widened and the blood drained from his face. 'He isn't luring us *to* him, he's luring us *away*!'

'Because he's not after us—'

'He's after Wolf.'

The reindeer threw down its head and charged at Wolf, who dodged its head-branches and darted round to nip its heels. Whitethroat, his less experienced pack-brother, leapt straight at its chest. The reindeer attacked with both

6

forelegs, kicking Whitethroat nose over tail into a drift – then fled through the trees and galloped off along the frozen Fast Wet.

Whitethroat scrambled out of the drift and made to give chase, but Wolf shot him a glance: *Let it go!* The reindeer was too healthy and strong, not worth risking a spike in the guts.

Embarrassed, Whitethroat nuzzled under Wolf's chin to say sorry for spoiling the hunt, and Wolf gave him a reassuring soft-bite on the ear. *You learn. We go on.* Together they trotted up the slope to catch the smells.

The Hot Bright Eye was rising in the Up, and magpies were clattering about in the pines, snapping twigs for their nests. Wolf liked the time of the Bright Soft Cold, as the drifts made it easier to trap prey. And all was well with the pack. Tall Tailless and the pack-sister were hunting in the next valley, and Pebble and Blackear were guarding the Den. Darkfur was in a bad mood. She always was when her belly was full of cubs, but Wolf knew that if he tried to help her dig she would only growl at him and kick out furious spurts of earth.

The wind carried the scent of beaver: Whitethroat was eagerly sniffing. He was a fast runner, but young and not very clever. He still hadn't learnt that if you tried to dig a beaver from under the Bright Hard Cold, it simply swam away.

Suddenly Wolf caught a new scent that made his claws tighten and his hackles bristle. *Demon.*

Wolf knew in a snap that this wasn't one of the lesser demons that lurk in shadows and can be swiftly chased underground. This demon was cunning and immensely powerful. It stalked the Forest as a pale-pelted tailless, and in the past it had attacked Wolf and Tall Tailless and the pack-sister.

And this time it was horribly near the Den.

TWO

Torak crested the ridge. From where he stood, pines marched down to the white snake of the Elk River far below. Upstream and to his right, the valley narrowed, and the rapids at the Neck were a frozen tumult of ice. Above them on the other side of the river he saw the red rocks of the Den, where he and Renn were camped. All was eerily still beneath a heavy slate sky. No wolves. No Naiginn.

Renn pointed. 'There.'

Two grey blurs were streaking towards the Neck. Wolf and Whitethroat were racing flat out, and Torak knew at once that they weren't hunting prey, they were making for the Den. He and Renn started downhill, their snowshoes nightmarishly slow.

Already the two wolves had reached the Neck, their paws scarcely touching the ice as they flew across it. Whitethroat, being younger, was edging ahead. Suddenly he leapt into the air with a yelp and fell with an arrow jutting from his flank.

'Naiginn's in there!' shouted Renn, pointing at a thicket near the Den.

'We're after you, Naiginn!' yelled Torak, reaching behind him for an arrow as he ran. 'You'll never get out alive!'

Through the trees he caught a jolting glimpse of a man in seal hides bursting from the thicket. Pebble and Blackear were loping after him, but Naiginn was making for the river with viperous speed, twisting and turning on long bone skates and thrusting himself forwards by means of a spiked stick in either fist.

'I'm out of arrows!' yelled Renn. Torak whipped three from his quiver and she grabbed them – but she couldn't get a clear view for the trees.

It was all the time Naiginn needed. Gliding over the bank, he landed with a clatter on the frozen river and sped downstream. Wolf went hurtling after him.

Pack-brother, come back! howled Torak. But Wolf was unstoppable: hunting demons was what he was for.

Again and again Torak howled. Wolf and Naiginn were already out of sight.

Torak found Whitethroat staggering in circles, snapping at the arrowshaft jutting from his side. The wound didn't look mortal, it had missed his heart – so why was he dragging both hind legs in the snow?

As Torak and Renn reached him the young wolf's forelegs gave way and he collapsed in the snow. His tongue lolled. His tawny eye met Torak's in mute pleading: *Help me.*

'Why can't he move?' panted Torak.

Bent double with her hands on her knees, Renn shook her head.

Pebble emerged from the trees and hesitated, unsure whether to stay, or follow Wolf. Blackear ran to her stricken brother. The cleverer of the two, she often snapped at Whitethroat, but now she was licking his muzzle with frantic whines.

Whitethroat's eyelids trembled – then went still. Dullness crept over his eyes, like ice on a lake.

'He's dead,' Torak said in disbelief.

Blackear put up her muzzle and howled. Pebble joined in, their grief winding far into the hills.

Renn carefully drew the arrow from Whitethroat's flank and examined the wound. She studied the arrowhead's black flint tip. She sniffed it. She looked at Torak.

'What is it?' he said.

'Now we know why he couldn't move,' she said grimly. 'Wolfbane.'

Like all Forest people, Torak and Renn always carried what they needed for hunting, fire-making and sleep, so they didn't have to return to camp, and set off at once to find Wolf.

They had no use for snowshoes on the frozen river and the tracks were easy to follow: the scrape of Naiginn's skates, flanked by small rings pierced by a hole where he'd stabbed the ice with his sticks – and Wolf's big paw-prints flying after him. But Torak was painfully aware that even at a run they had no hope of catching their quarry.

He pictured Naiginn doubling back and lying in wait for Wolf. Surely Wolf was too wily to fall for such a trick? Surely he would smell Naiginn long before the demon sensed him, and evade an ambush?

The day wore on, and the breath of the World Spirit closed in around them, its freezing whiteness so thick that Torak couldn't see his outstretched hand. He'd howled himself hoarse calling for Wolf, but only once heard a distant reply: *Lost...* After that, silence. Torak told himself that if Wolf was lost in the fog, Naiginn would be too.

And now with the frost-fog came snow, softly and inexorably obliterating the trail. 'This is hopeless,' said Torak. 'I can hardly see a thing!'

'I don't know where we are,' said Renn. In summer they would have been able to hear the roar of the rapids at the Neck, but now Elk Valley was sunk in the hush of winter.

The only way to find him, Torak thought suddenly, is to spirit walk in a bird: soar above the Forest and scan with

12

a raven's far-seeing eyes. 'Where are Rip and Rek?' he said abruptly.

'I don't know.'

'Call them!'

'Torak,' Renn said sternly. 'You cannot spirit walk in a raven. You promised the wind you'd never fly again—'

'But this is *Wolf*!'

'Not even a raven could spot anything in this fog!'

'Then what do we do, just blunder about?'

'You're the best tracker in the Forest, you won't lose the trail!'

'I already have! Naiginn could've kept going downriver, or turned aside into the Forest, or...' He broke off, unable to voice the third possibility: that by now Wolf might be dead.

Wolfbane. In his mind Torak saw the plant's sinister hooded flowers. It grew throughout the Forest and beyond, and every part of it was lethal; the smallest child knew not to touch it. Until now, Torak had never reflected on what the name actually meant: *wolf-killer.*

In the Far North, hunters boiled its roots to a sticky sludge which they smeared on their harpoons, using just enough to immobilize a whale or a walrus; the poison wore off swiftly without tainting the flesh. Naiginn had been raised in the Far North by the Narwal Clan, he knew all about wolfbane. And he wanted Wolf alive – if only for a while: breathing yet helpless, so that he could feed...

13

From far upriver came the howls of what remained of the pack: the voices of Darkfur, Pebble and Blackear weaving together in a sorrowful, echoing song.

'What are they saying?' said Renn.

'Grieving for Whitethroat, calling for Wolf.' He frowned. 'Before we left, I told Pebble... I told him we'd find Wolf and bring him back.'

'And we will,' Renn said firmly.

He didn't reply. Wolves talk with their ears, tails and bodies as much as their voices, and their speech is subtle. Torak didn't speak it as well as a real wolf, but as he'd knelt by Whitethroat's body he'd managed to get across to Pebble and Blackear that they must return to the Den and guard Darkfur. Pebble had nuzzled his cheek so trustingly, believing that he would do what he said, and find Wolf.

What if I can't? thought Torak with a clutch of terror. What if I never see Wolf again?

On the bank Renn had gathered deadwood and was using her strike-fire to wake a small blaze.

'We're not stopping for the night!' he protested. 'Naiginn could be laying traps for Wolf right now, he could be—'

'He could be anywhere and so could Wolf: Torak, I know! That's why I'm doing a finding charm.' She'd reddened her brow with earthblood from her ravenskin medicine pouch, and was tucking a slip of dried auroch in the fork of an alder as an offering to her clan guardian.

Torak wrenched open his food pouch and left an

offering too, begging the Forest to look after Wolf. He wished he'd done it sooner.

Impatiently he watched Renn plant a tripod of sticks over the fire and hang a small tuft of grey fur on a withe, positioning the fur so that it turned slowly in the smoke, but didn't burn. She had flung back her hood and was watching the fur, her russet hair speckled with snow, her pale face rapt.

It was Wolf's underfur. The day before yesterday they'd played a game of tag, and Renn, breathless with laughter beneath a snuffling heap of wolves, had clawed at Wolf's belly while he gave her a thorough face-licking. She must have kept the underfur she'd pulled out. It was eerie how there were days when she seemed to know in advance what she would need for a charm, even if at the time she didn't know why.

'What's it telling you?' said Torak.

The intensity of her silence made the hairs on his forearms prickle. 'He's not in the Forest,' she said slowly, 'or on the river.'

'How can that be? There's nowhere else.'

'But that's what it says.' She frowned. 'Maybe it means he's reached the coast.'

'Wolf hates the Sea, he wouldn't go near it!'

'I know.'

Torak flung up his arms. 'So where is he?'

Wolf didn't know where he was. First the fog, and now the Bright Soft Cold, falling thickly from the Up.

He'd lost the demon's scent many lopes ago, and to his alarm, he could no longer smell the Forest. He'd howled himself hoarse, but he couldn't hear Tall Tailless or the others in the pack.

As he padded on, he caught a scent that made his pelt prickle with dread. It was a cold and ancient smell: the smell of the Great Wet. Wolf turned and headed the other way. In the past he and Tall Tailless had journeyed over the Great Wet in floating hides, and the memory was very bad. The Great Wet had no muzzle, yet she was never silent; limbless, yet endlessly moving, she was terrible in her sudden rages and her limitless power.

Fog swirled mockingly around Wolf. Somewhere a raven cawed. It wasn't one of the ravens who belonged to his pack. He let out a dispirited whine.

He came to a jagged hill covered in Bright Hard Cold and ran to the top to catch the smells. A chill wind blew back his fur, and in the distance he heard lapping and sucking, and a loud grinding, like some huge creature crunching bones.

Suddenly there was an ear-splitting crack and his hill tilted, nearly throwing him off. Wolf ran to the bottom. Another deafening crack. Beneath his paws the ground was rocking, and before him a black line was opening up.

In a tail-flick the black line had widened to an unleapable stretch of glistening black Wet. Should he

16

swim across? The Wet was growling, it would swallow him if he tried.

The wind was gusting fiercely now, clawing at the fog. Wolf saw the spiky darkness of the Forest, frighteningly far off. In it he made out tiny sparks of light. He knew those sparks, they were the Bright Beasts-that-Bite-Hot of taillesses. But both the Forest and the Dens of the taillesses were dropping away, and around him lay a vast, heaving expanse of black Wet, dotted with spikes of Bright Hard Cold.

Terror sank its teeth into Wolf's belly. This wasn't *land* he was standing on, it was a lump of Bright Hard Cold – and the wind was blowing him away from the Forest, over the Great Wet!

A howl rose in Wolf's throat. It ended in a whimper.

The Forest had disappeared. And the wind was still blowing him further and further over the Great Wet.

THREE

Kittiwakes were wailing and swooping over the ice-bergs in the bay, and the wind off the Sea was making Torak's cheekbones ache.

Grinding his teeth, he prowled the camp of the Sea-eagle Clan. Their shelters were glaring humps of fresh snow, most of them empty, as everyone was out at the fishing grounds. On the drying racks, herrings stared at him with dull dead eyes. It felt like an omen.

Last night in the fog, he and Renn had encountered a Raven Clan hunting party. Renn had wanted to go with them and consult her uncle, Fin-Kedinn, but they'd told her he wasn't in camp, he'd gone to the coast to trade furs for flint with the Sea-eagles. Torak and Renn had trudged on down the frozen river.

It was dawn by the time they'd reached the coast. By then the snow and fog had given way to clear skies and a hard frost, the cold so intense their breath crackled in their nostrils. Fin-Kedinn had been in the main shelter with the Elders. Torak had snatched a brief word with him, but hadn't seen him since. Would he *never* come out?

Squinting in the sun, Torak spotted Renn and their friend Dark, the Raven Mage. They were high on the headland overlooking the bay, helping Watash the Sea-eagle Mage do yet another finding charm. They'd been up there for ages, and still no sign of an answer.

'Why'd you need *another* one?' Torak had protested.

'Because,' Renn had snapped, 'this wretched cut on my hand is hindering my Magecraft. And three Mages are better than one!'

At the edge of camp Torak found a group of women scraping seal hides. 'Have you seen a lone wolf?' he asked. 'Black mane around his shoulders, missing the tip of his tail...'

They shook their heads. And, no, they hadn't seen a fair-haired hunter with a scarred face and Narwal clan-tattoos. Same answer he'd got from the Ravens last night – and from Fin-Kedinn and Dark. Wolf was long gone, Torak could feel it. But *where*? And was Naiginn still on his trail?

Torak was tormented by the fear that he'd missed the trail in the fog, and Wolf was somewhere in the Forest, hunted by an ice demon with a quiverful of poisoned arrows...

On the Point the three Mages had stretched pale gutskin over a light driftwood kite to make an eagle with outspread wings. Renn was giving it eyes with a stick of charcoal, and Dark was tying a long cord of twisted kelp to its foot. His strange snowy hair was streaming in the wind. Ark, his companion and spirit guide, was soaring overhead.

Torak gazed at the white raven with longing. Why bother doing a charm when he could spirit walk in Ark? All he needed was a smoke-potion to loosen his souls, or a bite of the black root which he *knew* Renn had in her medicine pouch.

But last night when he'd asked her she'd flatly refused. 'No, Torak, no! You broke your word to the wind once, you won't get away with it again!'

Behind the Elders' shelter he found Fin-Kedinn's dog sled. His dogs lay nearby, chewing bones. A brindled bitch heaved herself to her feet and came to greet Torak, but her puppy hung back, alarmed by his smell of wolves. Torak's heart contracted. The puppy was about three moons old, the same age Wolf had been when he'd found him.

Torak had been twelve when his father was killed by the bear. That night – his first dreadful night without Fa – he'd stumbled on a bedraggled little wolf cub yowling for his pack. Dead wolves lay about him in the mud, drowned by a flash flood which had destroyed their Den.

Wolf had been with Torak ever since. Together they'd hunted their first deer, and battled demons and Soul-Eaters;

and found mates. The bond between them was so strong that sometimes Torak had only to think about going hunting and Wolf would appear, ears pricked, eyes alight with eagerness: *Let's go!*

On the Point the gutskin eagle was ready to fly. Torak watched Renn put her lips close to it and mouth: *Where is Wolf?*

Watash the Sea-eagle Mage lifted the kite and let the wind carry it skywards, while Dark skilfully played out its tether. All three Mages stood watching its dizzying swoops and sudden faltering stillnesses.

Torak had almost given up hope when Renn's face changed. She called to him, but the wind whipped her voice away. Now she and Dark were running down the slope.

'West!' she panted, pointing over the waves.

'*What?*' cried Torak. 'Out to *Sea?*'

'We think so, yes!' said Dark.

'You *think* so?' shouted Torak. 'But what's it *mean?* Is he drowned? Eaten by a shark? Taken by Naiginn? *What?*'

'We don't know,' Dark said unhappily.

'That's all the charm told us,' said Renn.

'So much for Magecraft!' spat Torak, staring at the icebergs and wind-tossed waves that stretched all the way to the sky. Beyond the skyline lay the Seal Islands, and beyond them nothing but more Sea, on and on for ever... Wolf could be anywhere.

Renn came to stand beside him. 'We'll find him,' she said.

'If he's still alive. Your charm didn't tell us that.'

She bit her lip. 'I asked Watash if we could borrow a boat. She says they're all out at the herring grounds.'

He opened his mouth to reply, but at that moment the hides covering the low entrance to the Elders' shelter parted and Fin-Kedinn emerged.

Torak didn't wait for his foster father to stand. 'Wolf's somewhere at Sea, you *have* to make them give us a boat!'

Grasping his staff, the Raven Leader straightened up, his other hand clamped to the old wound in his thigh. 'There's something you need to hear,' he said.

'Fin-Kedinn, *please*, we need a boat!'

'Be silent,' the Raven Leader said in a voice that brooked no opposition.

For the first time Torak noticed another man behind Fin-Kedinn. He had stumpy arms and legs and stood no taller than an eight-year-old child, but his face was windburnt and capable and his shrewd eyes held the waterlight of a lifetime spent at Sea. 'This is Apsu, Elder of the Sea-eagle Clan,' said Fin-Kedinn. 'And Kujai, his son.'

The boy who'd followed them out was tall and well-built. He looked about Torak's own age, with what appeared to be a red stain on his cheek, and a thunderous scowl.

'Kujai,' said Fin-Kedinn, 'thinks he saw Wolf.'

'Where?' cried Renn and Torak together.

The young man shrugged. 'I was coming back from the herring grounds, spotted it on an iceberg. I thought it was a dog—'

'What was he doing?' broke in Torak. 'Was he alive?'

'I couldn't see, it was too far off, and getting dark.'

'Why didn't you rescue him?' demanded Torak.

Kujai glared at him.

'Was anyone after him?' said Renn.

'I don't know about *after* him,' the boy said sulkily. 'I was in sight of the Point when I passed a man in a skinboat. He asked if I'd seen a wolf, I said yes.'

'Why'd you tell him?' exploded Torak.

'Because he *asked*!' snapped Kujai. Glowering, he hacked at the snow with his heel. 'And I did *try* to rescue the wolf, but like I said, it was too far off and *it was dark*!'

Torak chewed his knuckles. 'We've got to find him before Naiginn does. Apsu, *please* – we *have* to have a boat!'

'And my people,' the Elder said drily, 'have to have fish.'

Torak made to reply, but Fin-Kedinn quelled him with a glance. He turned to Apsu. 'Two moons ago, this wolf saved the Forest. He helped bring back the First Tree after the Thunderstar struck.'

Apsu's eyes narrowed skeptically. 'Did you see that yourself?'

'No,' conceded Fin-Kedinn.

'We did!' cried Renn, Torak and Dark together.

The Elder scrutinized each of them in turn. At last he gave a curt nod and spoke to his son. 'Kujai, we have to do this.'

'*No!*' shouted his son.

'Do it,' said his father.

23

Again the boy dug at the snow with his heel. 'Yes, Fa,' he mumbled.

Apsu turned to Torak and Renn. 'My son has been making a canoe. It's almost finished. Help him get it seaworthy, and you can take it and find your wolf.'

FOUR

While Renn and Torak were in the shelter being given seaworthy gear, Fin-Kedinn sent Dark with Kujai to help finish the canoe.

The Sea-eagle boy didn't bother to wait for him and was already striding towards the woods. As he caught up, Dark asked where they were going. 'Boat shed,' the young man growled. 'How many canoes have you made?'

'None.'

'*None?* Why'd Fin-Kedinn think you can help?'

'I don't know. I'm quite good at carving.'

'Pff!'

Dark sucked in his lips. This was going to be fun.

They came to a cave in the hillside; he guessed this was the 'boat shed'. At the entrance a small boy was tending a fire and a steaming cooking-skin; he cast Kujai a shy, admiring glance. A dog sprang from its bed of spruce boughs and wagged its tail. Ark perched in a pine and glared at the dog.

Ducking his head to enter, Dark found himself ankle-deep in wood shavings, inhaling the sharp clean tang of tree-blood. Above him reared a wooden canoe big enough to hold six people. Its rear end swept upwards to a high, fish-shaped stern. Its looming prow was carved like a wolf's head with eagerly pricked ears. Dark was impressed. He said so.

Kujai shrugged his broad shoulders. 'I learnt by watching Fa. He's the best canoe-maker in the clans.'

'But it looks finished.'

Kujai snorted. 'Shows how much you know! I'll do the hull, you oil the inside. Start with the thwarts.'

'The what?' said Dark.

Kujai glared at him. 'Is that a joke?'

'No.'

'Haven't you ever seen a canoe?'

"Course I have. The Ravens' deerhide ones, Boar Clan dugouts, your seal-hide ones—'

'We only use them in summer. And Boar Clan dugouts are nothing *like* our canoes!'

Dark bristled. The Boar Clan had been wiped out by the Thunderstar. They deserved pity, not scorn.

'This,' snarled Kujai, slapping a plank fitted across the

canoe's belly, 'is a *thwart*! And *this*,' he snatched a stick wadded with rawhide and plunged it into the cooking-skin, 'is seal oil! Rub it in well. I'll finish the hull. Got it?'

'Got it,' muttered Dark.

They worked in prickly silence. After a while Dark glanced at Kujai. He was scorching sections of hull with a torch, then scouring off the charred bits with a scrap of rough grey hide. It was going to take all day. Dark pictured Torak's impatience.

'So if Renn and Torak are your friends,' Kujai said at last, 'why aren't you going with them?'

'I've never been to Sea, I'd only slow them down.'

With his forearm Kujai pushed back his unruly fair hair. 'Are they a mated pair?'

'Yes.'

'D'you have a mate?'

'No. How'd you get that stain on your cheek?'

'Birthmark,' Kujai said curtly. 'And that's only about the hundredth time someone's asked me.'

Dark blew out a long breath.

'Talking of marks...' Kujai indicated the clan-tattoo on Dark's forehead, a ring of thirteen small red dots. 'What's a Swan Clan boy doing with the Ravens?'

'Living with them,' snapped Dark. 'I was born without colour so my clan chucked me out. And that's only about the hundredth time someone's asked *me*!'

'I didn't ask. You told me.'

'Well, now you know.'

'Fine.'

'Fine.'

The day dragged on. Dark finished oiling the inside and Kujai tossed him the grey hide – he called it sharkskin – and told him to help with the hull. Dark turned the hide in his fingers. 'What *is* a shark?'

'Don't you know ANYTHING?' roared Kujai.

'Not about the Sea, no!' retorted Dark. 'I grew up in the Mountains! Why are you so angry?'

'Because I've been working on this canoe since *last spring*!'

Ark flew off with a squawk. The dog slunk away. The boy tending the cooking-skin went to hide behind a pine.

'A canoe,' said Kujai, struggling to master his temper, 'is a living thing. Do you have any idea what it takes to make one?'

Dark crossed his arms on his chest and glowered at the fire.

'You've got to find the perfect lime tree and make sure that it wants to *be* a canoe. You've got to strip the trunk and soak it in a marsh to make it supple. Then you spend moon after moon hollowing it out: burning it with hot rocks, adzing off the charcoal, burning some more, till it's no thicker than three fingers wide on the bottom, and two on the sides. After that you stretch its belly using more hot rocks, and steam, and *thwarts*! You carve the prow and stern separately, fix them on with pegs so they won't ever come off. *All winter* I've worked on it! And now you and your friends come along and—'

'All*right*!' yelled Dark. 'But just so you know, Renn was fostered with the Whale Clan and Torak learnt skinboating with the Seals, so they'll look after your precious boat and you'll get it back!'

'No, I won't!'

'Yes, you will, they've been to Sea before—'

'That was in *summer*! Spring's the *worst time*!'

Dark put his hands on his hips. 'What d'you want me to do now?'

'Oil the stern.'

'Right.' The stern was shaped like a leaping fish with a blunt nose and a tall dorsal fin. Privately, Dark had to admit that Kujai was a pretty good carver.

The Sea-eagle boy saw him admiring it. 'I bet you don't know what those carvings are for,' he said.

'I can guess,' said Dark. 'The wolf at the front helps you see where you're going. The fish at the back wards off danger from behind.'

Kujai raised his eyebrows. 'Finally, he gets something right! Though it's not a fish, it's a Sea wolf.'

Dark sighed. 'And I've no idea what that is.'

Kujai's lip curled. 'Some clans call them Hunters, but we use the old name. They're black and white, incredibly fast, not afraid of anything.'

'How big?'

'Bigger than a dolphin, smaller than a whale. Which probably means nothing to you as you've never seen either.'

Dark laughed.

'Sea wolves are sacred,' added Kujai. 'That's really why Fa's helping your friends find their wolf.'

'But – Wolf isn't a Sea wolf, he's a wolf.'

'Same thing. When a wolf walks into the Sea, it turns into a Sea wolf. When a Sea wolf comes ashore, it turns into a wolf. Two bodies, one spirit. Understand?'

'So... the Sea wolves will help Wolf?'

'Oh, no, Sea wolves hunt everything!'

'Do they eat people?'

'If they get in the way.'

Dark was reaching inside his medicine pouch. 'I'm going to rub earthblood on the hull to protect my friends.'

Kujai was startled. 'That's the last step. How did you know?'

'I am a Mage,' Dark said drily.

Kujai took a birch-bark bowl of reddish-brown powder and was about to tip it into the remaining seal oil when Dark stopped him. 'Let's use mine.' He held up a chunk.

Kujai's jaw dropped. 'I've *heard* of purple earthblood but I've never seen any. Where'd you get it?'

'In a cave. So what do you think? Shall we put some on the hull?'

Torak woke before dawn. He'd dreamt that Naiginn was wearing Wolf's pelt and laughing. Wolf's shrivelled forepaws dangled on the demon's chest. Wolf's eyes were empty slits in his mangled head.

Cold rasped Torak's lungs as he crawled outside. The sky was still dark and the First Tree was shimmering, its luminous boughs turning the snow faintly green. The drift ice in the bay had congealed to a patchwork of pale floes seamed with dark new ice. When they set off they'd have to break through it, unless the tide did it for them.

'Ice is Naiginn's element,' Renn said quietly at his elbow. 'Looks like it's helping him.' Her face was drawn and she was flexing her injured hand inside her mitten. He asked if the cut was worse but she shrugged it off. 'I sent Rip and Rek to find Wolf,' she told him. 'Not sure if they'll obey. You never know with ravens.'

Torak stared out to Sea. 'Naiginn's got at least a day's lead on us and he's the best skinboater in the Far North—'

'And the Sea is vast, and he doesn't know which way Wolf went. At least we do.'

'But—'

'Wolf is alive, Torak.'

'How do you *know*?'

'I don't, not for sure. But the finding charm said "he is in the west". I think that gives us hope.'

The camp was waking up, torches flaring orange in the gloom. Apsu and the Elders stood on the shore, scanning Sea and sky for weather signs. Kujai and his brothers were trudging into the woods to fetch the canoe. Renn said, 'I'm going to find Dark and make an offering to the Sea Mother.'

31

'Be quick,' muttered Torak.

One delay after another, he thought as he paced the snow. The *moment* Wolf went after Naiginn I should have gone after them. No stopping to comfort Whitethroat, no saying goodbye to Blackear and Pebble. If only I'd been more ruthless. More like Naiginn...

Spotting Fin-Kedinn, Torak ran after him and drew him aside. 'Take this,' he said in an undertone, pressing his medicine horn into his foster father's hand.

Fin-Kedinn was aghast. 'You can't leave this behind!' The horn was made from a tine of the World Spirit's antler – and doubly precious as it had been carved by Torak's mother.

'Look after it,' Torak insisted. 'For safe-keeping.'

With his forefinger the Raven Leader traced the Forest mark incised on the horn's polished black surface. His vivid blue gaze pierced Torak's souls. 'You're not leaving this for safe-keeping,' he said in a low voice. 'This horn – and the spirit of she who made it – keeps you steady. But you don't want to be steady. You want to be without mercy. Like the demon you hunt.'

'Keep it safe,' said Torak. 'And don't tell Renn!'

Dark was helping Torak and Kujai load the canoe, and Renn had slipped off to change the binding on her hand.

She'd tried willow bark and pounded juniper berries, and wormwood to drive away demons, but nothing had worked. The wound was oozing yellow pus and the swelling had spread, the pain so fierce that she could hardly clench her fist. Hurriedly she applied a poultice of crushed sorrel root, then a soft pad of horsehoof mushroom tied on with buckskin.

Behind her the pines were still violet shadows, but above the Forest the crimson glow of sunrise was softening to orange. The wind was blowing from the north, and the ice in the bay was breaking up. Renn couldn't remember if the tide was coming in or going out. Last night she and Torak had struggled to take in everything the Sea-eagles told them about currents and submerged rocks, riptides, Sea wolves, and islands with beaches of treacherous quicksand...

'How's your hand?' said Fin-Kedinn, making her jump.

'Better,' she lied.

He snorted. 'Is that why you're leaving your bow with Dark?'

She shrugged. 'Salt water wouldn't do it any good.'

'Hmm. Did you sleep?'

'Not much. I was thinking about Wolf.' Several winters ago, she had been carried away on an ice floe. She remembered the deadly black water around her, and the dreadful sense of helplessness.

Torak was beckoning to them, and they started towards the canoe. Renn noticed that Fin-Kedinn's limp was worse. In the grey dawn light she saw the silver in his dark-red hair and beard; shadows under his eyes, lines at the sides

33

of his mouth. 'How long has the pain been this bad?' she asked.

'Watash gave me a salve. It's bound to help.'

Renn wasn't convinced. Her uncle had got the wound five winters ago fighting the demon bear, and she'd tried every cure she knew. So had Dark. Nothing had worked.

'Let's swap wrist-guards,' Fin-Kedinn said briskly. 'I had Dark put a charm on mine, it'll help heal your cut.'

'Don't change the subject,' she said with a curl of her lip.

He chuckled. 'You're a fine one to talk, pretending your hand doesn't hurt!'

As they paused to tie the wrist-guards on each other's forearms, Fin-Kedinn said, 'Torak told me that when Naiginn attacked the wolves, the two of you shot at him.'

'Of course.'

'Do I need to remind you that Naiginn is your half-brother? That killing your bone kin is forbidden by clan law?'

'No, but—'

'Kill Naiginn and you become outcast, Renn. You couldn't ever be with Torak again. Or with me.'

'I know that.'

'But you're determined to do it anyway, to stop Torak being outcast – just as Torak, who is also Naiginn's bone kin, is determined to protect *you*.'

Renn did not reply. Sometimes Fin-Kedinn saw too much.

'I intend to find a way to destroy the demon without *either* of you killing him,' he said with quiet intensity. 'I want you *both* back – and not as outcasts. That's all I care about!'

Renn tried to speak, but there was a lump in her throat. She felt eight summers old again. Her fa had just been killed on the ice river, and Fin-Kedinn had promised to look after her. He'd kept his word. She wanted to believe that he would find a way to destroy Naiginn without anyone becoming outcast, but she couldn't see it.

Torak was calling to them from the canoe, desperate to be off.

Suddenly Renn caught movement at the edge of the Forest. She breathed in with a hiss. Among the trees a white elk stood watching them. White elks are rare, and to see one is a bad sign. Renn wondered if it meant that something had happened to Wolf.

'Renn, come *on*!' shouted Torak. 'The days are short enough without wasting half the morning!'

The white elk turned and vanished into the Forest. Fin-Kedinn's hard features were inscrutable as he watched it go. 'Torak's right,' he murmured. 'The days are short.'

Glancing down at Renn, his face softened, and he drew her against him and held her tight. She shut her eyes and sniffed his smell of woodsmoke and reindeer hide. 'Come back soon,' he told her. 'May the guardian fly with you.'

At last she and Torak were in the canoe and heading out to Sea, Torak kneeling in the bow, wielding the double-bladed paddle, Renn in the stern, gripping the steering-paddle with her good hand.

The instant they passed the Point the wind strengthened and so did the swell, pitching them up and down. Renn twisted round and saw Fin-Kedinn and Dark standing on the shore. It seemed to her that they were the ones being carried away. She wondered if she would ever see them again.

Before her stretched the open Sea: unknowable, immeasurably vast. Wolf was out there at the mercy of the Sea Mother – except that the Sea Mother *had* no mercy. She was so powerful that her breathing in and out made the tides. If she was pleased, she sent whales and seals to be hunted. If not, she sent storms that ravaged camps and dragged fishing boats to their doom.

Over his shoulder Torak said, 'I can't feel him, Renn. I can't sense Wolf at all.'

'He's too far away. It doesn't mean he's dead.'

'I can't bear to think of him on that iceberg! What if he thinks we've abandoned him?'

'Oh, Torak, he must know we're looking for him!'

He turned round. The scar on his cheek was livid and his light-grey eyes were haunted. 'That's what I tell myself – but what if he doesn't? What if he thinks we're not coming?'

fIVE

Wolf was cold, wet and lonely — but not for a tail-flick did he doubt that Tall Tailless was coming to find him.

I never leave you, Tall Tailless had told him once. And whenever Wolf was in trouble, Tall Tailless had rescued him. Even when bad taillesses had taken Wolf far from the Forest and stamped on his tail, his pack-brother had found him and set him free.

In his head Wolf saw Tall Tailless and the pack-sister racing over the Great Wet in their floating hide. They were coming for him, he was sure of it.

But when?

He could catch no smells on the wind. No sounds

except the splash and suck of waves, and the Bright Hard Cold crackling and growling beneath his paws. He could see no birds in the Up. No land anywhere. Nothing but the endless, heaving Great Wet.

Waves drenched him, spray stung his eyes. He shook himself and nearly fell over. And this rocking was making him sick.

Thirsty, he snapped at the little chunks of Bright Hard Cold lying about on his hill. The last one looked a bit like a lemming, so he patted it with his forepaw. It slithered away and he chased it, the chunk nimbly evading his pounces – until it shot into the Wet and refused to come back.

Still thirsty, he gnawed the edge of his Bright Hard Cold. It tilted alarmingly, almost throwing him off. It didn't like being bitten. He decided not to do it again.

Putting up his muzzle, he howled, but he sounded so alone that he stopped.

Suddenly he caught the distant shrieks of fish-birds. Scrambling to the top of his Bright Hard Cold, he strained eyes and ears and nose.

There they were, diving after fish!

As Wolf drifted nearer, he heard strange rattling clicks in the deeps, and long wavering howls. He knew those howls, he remembered them from before. They were the big black-and-white fish that hunted in packs, like wolves.

They were clever, the wolves of the Wet. In the distance Wolf saw them diving to chase the fish to the surface, stunning them by thrashing the waves with their tails, chomping them in their powerful jaws – while above them fish-birds shrieked and fought for scraps.

And now even *bigger* fish were joining the hunt! Enormous as mountains, flailing flippers longer than trees, their huge black heads spouted great jets of spray as they opened cavernous mouths to swallow whole shoals.

Wolf's pelt tightened with fear. He had hunted musk-oxen and bison, he'd fought bears and bad taillesses and demons – and yet against these hunters of the Great Wet he was as helpless as a newborn cub.

But soon the hunt was over. The mountainfish and the wolves of the Wet disappeared and the deeps fell silent. The fish-birds flew off. All that remained were a few scraps floating on the foam.

A fish tail drifted past Wolf's Bright Hard Cold and his hunger came roaring back. If he jumped in after it, would he be able to scramble back?

A sleek head bobbed up and grabbed the tail in its muzzle. Lazily the fish-dog rolled onto its back, gripping its prize in its flippers and munching, its round eyes taunting Wolf: *I have fish, you don't!*

Suddenly Wolf's Bright Hard Cold bumped against something and he forgot all about the fish-dog. *He had reached land!*

It was a knobbly, treeless little island of black rock, but it was land, and he leapt eagerly ashore. The rocks felt slippery and oddly soft beneath his paws – and with an ear-biting Pssh! a huge jet of Wet exploded right in front of his nose. Wolf hurtled back onto his Bright Hard Cold. The 'island' uttered another Pssh! as the mountainfish raised one long flipper – then its vast tail rose briefly into the Up and it dived into the deep.

Shaken, Wolf staggered about on his Bright Hard Cold. To calm himself he lapped the Wet. It tasted horrible and only made him thirstier.

Miserably he slumped onto his belly. What if Tall Tailless wasn't coming? What if he *couldn't* come? What if the pale-pelted demon had killed him and the pack-sister?

The Hot Bright Eye was rising in the Up, glaring down at Wolf. The rocking was making him dizzy...

In the Now that he goes to in his sleeps, he is a cub again, safe in the Den, and his mother is licking his belly. Now he is play-stalking Tall Tailless: sneaking up and knocking him over, and his pack-brother is yelping and baring his blunt little teeth, which is his way of laughing. And somewhere, wolf cubs are whining...

Wolf cubs?

Wolf started awake.

He heard wingbeats, and in the Up he saw two distant specks. Wolf leapt to his feet, barking and lashing his tail, so happy he nearly fell into the Wet. Two ravens were flying towards him – and they were *his* ravens, the ones who belonged to the pack! This *must* mean that Tall Tailless and the pack-sister were coming!

The ravens lit onto the Bright Hard Cold and stalked about, whining like wolf cubs, as they often did to tease him. Wolf was whimpering and waggling his hindquarters, trying to tell them what had happened, and they were hopping sideways and fluttering out of his way, giving no sign that they understood.

Perched on top of the Bright Hard Cold, they peered down at him. Cark! Then they hitched their wings and flew away.

Filled with new hope, Wolf waited for them to return. Surely they had gone to fetch Tall Tailless!

The Hot Bright Eye rolled across the Up. Tall Tailless didn't come.

For the first time since Wolf had been carried off from the Forest, he remembered that his pack-brother was not a real wolf. Tall Tailless couldn't see in the dark, and he could hardly smell or hear at all. So how, in the endless Great Wet, could he possibly find Wolf?

Wolf sat on his haunches, too discouraged even to whine. He heard the Wet gnawing at his Bright Hard Cold. He thought of Darkfur and Pebble, Whitethroat and Blackear. He missed them so much it hurt.

What if Darkfur couldn't manage when the cubs came, and Wolf wasn't there to catch prey for them, and chase away bears?

Suddenly Wolf became aware of a distant clicking, and long wavering howls, like those of a wolf pack – but not.

Lurching to his feet, he padded to the edge.

41

In the deep, only a pounce from where he stood, he made out a pale, glimmering spot. It was growing steadily bigger. Rising towards him.

Panting with alarm, Wolf backed away. The wolves of the Wet had returned.

With leisurely ease, a big blunt head poked above the waves. Wolf saw the creature's pale belly as it reared out of the Wet. He saw the white patch behind its eye: the keen dark eye that watched him intently – then sank slowly out of sight.

Wolf fled to the other side of the Bright Hard Cold. Some distance away, another wolf of the Wet rose briefly to study him. Then another. And another.

Wolf knew exactly why they were doing this because he'd done it himself many times when he was hunting.

The wolves of the Wet were taking a good look at their prey.

SIX

The canoe handled better than Torak had dared
hope. Its wide belly made it steadier than a skinboat,
and the high wolf's-head prow cut through rough water
and shielded them from spray. But the wind was against
them, blowing hard in their faces, and it was noon by the
time they reached the herring grounds.

Everywhere they looked, canoes were bobbing on silver
waves that flashed and glinted with fish. Gulls screamed
and swooped. In the distance they saw the misty spouts
of whales.

Most of the Sea-eagles were too busy raking in

herrings to talk, but one man said he'd spotted 'a dog on an iceberg'.

'Which way was it heading?' cried Torak, bringing their canoe alongside.

'I didn't look.' Frowning with concentration, the fisherman dragged his rake through the shoal, its bone barbs snagging a wriggling row of fish; he dropped them into the boat by rapping the rake on the side.

'Did you see a man in a skinboat?' said Renn.

The fisherman shook his head, but a girl in another canoe shouted: 'I saw the iceberg moving south-west! I think the current was taking it towards the Islands...'

'The Seal Islands?' yelled Torak.

The girl nodded. 'That's where the current goes!'

Torak and Renn exchanged glances. 'In the past we've made it to the Islands in a day,' said Renn. 'Maybe Wolf's already reached land.'

'If his iceberg didn't flip over,' said Torak. 'Or if the current didn't sweep him past the Islands and even further out to Sea. If, if, if!'

A shark glided under the boat, its flat eye meeting his as it powered through the water with snake-like thrusts. He pictured his pack-brother bravely swimming, the shark closing in with gaping jaws... But even a shark, Torak reflected, would be preferable to what Naiginn would do if he caught Wolf.

'Let's keep heading west,' said Renn.

'Nothing else we can do,' he muttered.

He knew his way around Seal Island, but he'd never been on Cormorant Island or even seen the island of the Kelps. *If* Wolf had reached the Islands, he could be on any of them – or on one of the many islets that dotted the Sea.

The sky clouded over, and soon sleet was stinging their faces, although thanks to the Sea-eagles they stayed warm and dry. They'd been given over-parkas and leggings of light waterproof gutskin, fish-skin gauntlets lined with reindeer hide, and thigh-length seal-hide boots. To shut out the glare, Torak wore his eyeshield of pale polished antler, but Renn's eyeshield was new. Its narrow slits made her inscrutable, and as it was made of black whale bone – the same material which Naiginn had used for traps in the Deep Forest – it was a disturbing reminder that the ice demon was her half-brother.

She tapped his shoulder, making him jump. 'Did you hear that?'

Resting his paddle across his knees, he paused to listen. From far down in the deep came faint whistles and long eerie shrieks. He recognized them. They were made by the great black-and-white fish which he and Renn knew as Hunters, but which Apsu called Sea wolves. Torak had been chased by one once. It had nearly got him.

After a while the sounds faded to nothing. Renn breathed out. 'I think they're gone.'

He nodded. 'Sounded as if they were hunting.'

The day wore on and he paddled till his shoulders

screamed for rest and his eyes ached from scanning the Sea. Still no Wolf. Just a scattering of icebergs and gull-haunted islets. We're getting nowhere, thought Torak. I *have* to spirit walk in a gull and *fly*!

Renn was rummaging in her medicine pouch. 'Earthblood!' she muttered. 'I *knew* I'd forgotten something! How could I be so stupid? Chuck me your medicine horn, will you?'

'Later. We need to find somewhere to camp.'

'Why not now? I only need a pinch for my hand.'

'Sun's getting low, Renn. Keep an eye out for land!' He'd been putting off telling her that he'd left the horn with Fin-Kedinn. He couldn't put it off for much longer.

Soon afterwards she spotted a low island which looked as if it would do. On the leeward side they found a cove with rocks and a sweep of greenish sand backed by wind-bent trees. Near the rocks stood three small roe deer, munching seaweed and watching them.

As the tide was going in, Torak turned the boat in the way Kujai had advised, with its prow facing out to Sea, so that the incoming waves carried them shorewards. Suddenly Renn gave a shout: 'I think I see wolf tracks!'

'Where!'

'There, on the sand!' Already she'd jumped into the surf and was wading ashore.

The deer fled for the trees, and a pair of oystercatchers flew up from the rocks and circled the cove, objecting noisily to the intruders. Torak noticed that the deer hadn't

46

taken the shorter route across the sand, but had run *around* it. Then he spotted a battered spear planted by the rocks. Could it be a warning?

Belatedly he remembered the Sea-eagles' advice about quicksand. 'Renn, come back!' he yelled.

'I'm trying!' she shouted crossly, but she was wobbling calf-deep in sticky green mud.

'Don't struggle, you'll only sink deeper!'

'I know what they *said*,' she snapped, 'but it's a lot harder to do!'

'Here, grab the paddle!'

Luckily she was still within reach and he managed to pull her out, covered in stinking green slime and furious with herself. 'And after all that,' she complained, 'they weren't even tracks!'

They camped on a stretch of shingle above the rocks. Torak woke a driftwood fire and made a shelter by upending the canoe on shoresticks and packing more driftwood round the sides, while Renn cleaned her outer clothes and hung them to dry. The Sea-eagles had given them a pouch of smoked herrings, but as they were saving them, Torak went foraging on the rocks; he killed a big scarlet crab and gathered handfuls of purple seamoss and crunchy green oarweed.

As night fell it grew abruptly colder. Drift ice clinked in the shallows. The oystercatchers were still flying round and round, indignantly peeping.

Torak had seen no sign of Rip and Rek all day, and he

wondered if the ravens were avoiding him: if they'd sensed that he was desperate to spirit walk in them.

'I need that earthblood,' said Renn. 'Can I have your medicine horn?'

He looked at her steadily. 'I haven't got it. I left it with Fin-Kedinn.'

She was astonished. '*Why?*'

He hesitated. 'It felt as if it was holding me back.'

'From what?'

'All the things I'm not supposed to do.' Snatching a stick, he stabbed the fire. 'I'm not allowed to spirit walk in a bird. Can't kill my bone kin… Naiginn's not bound by any of it.'

'He's a demon, Torak. You're human.'

He threw aside the stick. 'To catch your prey, you've got to think like it.'

'But not become it!'

'There's no risk of that.'

'You're already at risk,' she said sternly. 'I've been thinking about it since we left the coast. All those laws you've broken in the past: breaking your oath, and your promise to the wind, naming the dead out loud… And spirit walking too, it leaves traces on your souls: the viper, the ice bear – the Soul-Eater.'

'I've spirit walked in the Forest. That must be good!'

'But the Forest has been weakened by the Thunderstar. Your spirit was already damaged, Torak. And now without the medicine horn… It never occurred to me before, but I think in some way it kept you balanced.'

Torak was shaken. He'd wondered this himself, but hearing her say it – and echoing Fin-Kedinn's words – made it more real.

'Well, it's gone now,' she sighed. Opening her medicine pouch, she took a pinch of yellow bloodstone and sprinkled it on her injured hand.

Torak couldn't take his eyes off the pouch in her lap. That pouch held the black root he needed to loosen his souls and spirit walk. And the oystercatchers were still flying.

Just *take* it! he thought suddenly. She can't stop you, you're bigger than her!

He lunged for it, but she'd seen the violence in him and scrambled to her feet.

'Give it to me!' he said between his teeth.

'What if you anger the wind into sending a storm? You'd get us both killed – and Wolf too!'

'I said give it to me!' He was advancing on her and she was backing away, her eyes were wide with shock.

A log exploded, sparks shooting at the stars.

What am I *doing*? thought Torak. This is *Renn*!

'I'm sorry,' he mumbled. Seaweed crunched beneath his boots as he stumbled down to the rocks. Above him hung the thin crescent moon. Before him the Sea lay black.

Gradually his heartbeats slowed and his blood stopped pounding in his ears. A thought slid into his mind. Once, I spirit walked in a fish... And in a seal. I knew what it was to be weightless and fast, so very very fast...

The answer was so simple that he almost laughed aloud. He didn't *need* to fly through the air, he could fly through the Sea!

And in the Sea lived stronger, fiercer creatures than seals.

SEVEN

'What's the strongest creature in the Sea?' whispered Dark.

'Hunter or prey?' replied Kujai in an undertone.

'Doesn't matter as long as it's the strongest.'

'A whale.'

'Draw one!'

The Sea-eagle boy saw that he was in earnest and grabbed a stick. The fish he drew in the snow had a great grooved belly and long narrow flippers; a downturned mouth, a tiny dorsal fin. 'Humpback whale. What's this about?'

'I have to make one fast! Help me find what I need.'

'Why?'

'Tell you later.'

'Tell me now!'

'Kujai, there isn't time!'

'Right. What d'you need?'

Torak and Renn had set out the day before, and Dark and Fin-Kedinn had remained at the Sea-eagle camp to finish their trade. That night Dark had dreamt he was underwater. In the blackness he was aware of a gliding menace. It wasn't after him, it was after Torak, Renn and Wolf. They were tumbling through the deep towards the Sea wolf's gaping jaws...

Dark had started awake, wheezing in horror. His friends were in more danger than they realized, he was sure of it. The only way to save them was Sea Magecraft, and though he knew nothing of the Sea, he felt in his marrow that Watash couldn't help. They were *his* friends, so he must work the charm.

It was past moonset when he'd woken Kujai and they'd crawled out of the shelter. To his relief the Sea-eagle boy asked no further questions and set about gathering what was needed.

The sky was prickling with stars but dawn wasn't far off when they reached the boat shed among the trees. While Kujai woke a fire, Dark unrolled a large piece of silver halibut skin and cut out two whale shapes the length of his forearm, and two long narrow flippers. Hastily he sewed the whale halves together with sinew, leaving a gap for stuffing it with seaweed, and putting a rock in its

52

belly to help it sink. After sealing the gap, he sewed on the flippers and added two mussel-shell eyes, so that the creature could find his friends.

Kujai was mixing hot fish-bone glue with the black stain from an octopus he'd speared on the rocks. Into this Dark crumbled earthblood, then he painted the grooves on the whale's belly which Kujai had described, and marks of power on its tail.

The effigy was ready. If it pleased the Sea Mother, she *might* send help.

'What do we do now?' said Kujai.

'We take it to the open Sea and send it on its way.'

'We'll need a boat. Leave that to me!'

The sky was growing lighter by the time they put out, Kujai steering his big brother's canoe between clinking shards of ice, Dark gripping the stuffed whale between his knees and clutching the sides of the boat.

The stars were fading, gulls flying past on their way to the fishing grounds. As they passed the Point, the canoe bucked in the swell and icy wind numbed Dark's face. He leant over the side and wished he hadn't. He couldn't see the bottom.

Kujai's white teeth gleamed. 'Don't tell me you're sea-sick!'

'Stop paddling,' muttered Dark. 'We've come far enough.'

Deftly Kujai steadied the canoe while Dark chanted the sending charm. Dawn was breaking, a crimson gash in the east. Was he too late? Had the Sea wolves already attacked?

It seemed an age till he reached the end of the charm, but at last he cast the whale head-first over the side. *Go to the Sea Mother*, he told it silently, watching the silver fish dive into darkness. *Save my friends!*

The wolves of the Wet had disappeared, but Wolf knew that they hadn't gone far. Though he could no longer hear their howls, he sensed their intent. They would be back. They were simply doing what all hunters do: waiting for hunger and fear to weaken the prey.

The Hot Bright Eye was rising in the Up, glaring at Wolf as he paced to and fro. He noticed with alarm that his Bright Hard Cold was smaller than before. Wet was trickling off its edges, and its once-jagged hill had dwindled to a smooth, slippery bump.

Suddenly the wind carried a familiar scent to Wolf's nose. *There.* Far away on the edge of the Great Wet: *land!*

This time Wolf smelt that it really *was* land, and not some mountainfish taking a nap. He caught the scent of rocks and bracken and actual trees. But between him and the land lay an unswimmable gulf. If only the Bright Hard Cold would carry him closer!

A wave sloshed over him, nearly knocking him off his feet. The Bright Hard Cold was *much* smaller, and he could hear the Great Wet gnawing its belly. Fear sank its teeth into his guts. Soon it would be gone.

And from down in the deep came the hunting howls of the wolves of the Wet.

Torak caught the clamour of seabirds and dug in his paddle. As the sun rose higher he spotted the flash of wings above a foaming stretch of Sea. Gulls and guille-mots were diving, gannets plummeting into the waves. He pictured whales hunting underwater.

'We're getting too close!' cried Renn, yanking the steering-paddle.

'No, keep it straight!' he shouted. 'I have to get nearer!' If he could spirit walk in a whale he'd have a much better chance of finding Wolf than lumbering about in this canoe.

The Sea was choppy, the boat leaping like a hare in spring-time – and the whales were still too far away. As he struggled to reach them, their spouts vanished and the seabirds flew off.

Torak stopped paddling and dipped one paddle blade in the water, putting the other to his ear.

'What are you doing?' Renn said suspiciously.

He motioned her to silence.

Dimly, through the noise of the Sea slapping the hull, he caught whistles and squeals, long wavering howls. He broke into a grin. These weren't just whales, they were

Sea wolves! 'That way!' he cried. Stabbing the waves with his paddle, he powered towards the sounds.

'What are you *doing?*' Renn shouted again.

In the distance he glimpsed misty spouts and tall black fins, gleaming backs arching out of the Sea. If he could spirit walk in the cleverest, *fastest* hunters in the deep, he was bound to find Wolf! He would find Naiginn too, he would dive beneath the ice demon's boat and toss him screaming into the air, he would catch him in his jaws and—

A throaty Pssh! and a drenching jet of spray exploded near the canoe. Another jet, and another... Now seven black-and-white Sea wolves were spouting in unison, whistling and squealing to one another as they raced the canoe.

Renn was gripping the steering-oar with her good hand, trying frantically to turn the boat.

'Stay with them!' shouted Torak, paddling as hard as he could. 'Give me your medicine pouch!'

'Spirit walk in a *Sea wolf?* Are you mad?'

'Quickly, they're getting away!'

Already the Sea wolves were many boat-lengths ahead – except for one, which had stayed behind. From its unscarred hide Torak guessed it was a youngster. It seemed inquisitive, poking its head above the waves to look at them. Playfully it slammed the waves with its flipper, nearly swamping the boat.

With his paddle Torak splashed back. Then he lunged at Renn. 'Give me the root!'

She fended him off with a kick. 'You could barely control a bear's souls, a Sea wolf's spirit would be ten times stronger!'

The Sea wolf was swimming upside down beneath the boat, showing its pale belly and blowing streams of bubbles that made the surface boil.

'Don't come any nearer!' Renn warned Torak. She made to chuck the pouch overboard but he grabbed her wrist and twisted. She screamed as he wrenched the pouch from her grip.

The Sea wolf was trailing a long strand of kelp in its jaws: *Let's play!*

Torak rummaged for the black root and crammed it in his mouth.

'Spit it out before it's too late!' hissed Renn, clutching her injured hand.

'I have to find Wolf!' he mumbled.

'What about me? If your souls get into that creature how will they ever get out? I'll be left with your body, watching you die! Adrift with a corpse on the open Sea!'

Torak opened his mouth to reply – and suddenly pain was wrenching his guts and his souls were tearing loose. Renn was calling his name but her voice was drowned in a gurgling rush, and he was powering into the deep with fast smooth strokes of his enormous tail.

He was weightless and warm and drunk with the joy of flying through his beautiful green Sea. He heard fish nibbling kelp, and cod grunting and barking. He heard the squeals of his brothers and sisters and the calls of his mother, who was leader of the pack. Thoughts flickered between them and he caught every meaning, every intent. He called back, sending a hailstorm of clicks into a vast, ever-changing web of sound.

Through a glittering rain of fish-scales, he saw a distant shoal of herring shivering like windblown grass. He made out gulls and guillemots flying fast through the water, and gannets flashing white wings to get away from him.

He realized that he wasn't seeing with his eyes, but with *sound*. He 'saw' frightened seals fleeing from him into the vast sun-dappled forest of kelp that shimmered and swayed below. He saw tiny silver capelin darting like swallows through the endless greeny-gold fronds, and prickly orange starfish, and anemones' purple tentacles probing wands of light. He was *inside* the sounds and they were thrilling through him, buzzing over his skin.

The Sea wolf's spirit was so strong that Torak forgot everything except the thrill of the chase and the urge to rejoin his pack. And now his mother was calling that the prey was growing weak, it was time for the kill. Already his brothers and sisters were excitedly tossing shrieks back and forth, and moving as one to surround it.

On impulse Torak rose to scan the world above. An uprush of bubbles, a blast of wind chilling his blunt black head as he burst spouting into the jagged air...

And deep in the Sea wolf's salty marrow, Torak came to himself with a jolt.

Through a haze of his pack-mates' spray he saw Renn grimacing in pain as she struggled to master the boat one-handed.

He saw a skinboat in the distance: Naiginn's fair hair streaming as he raced towards her with death in his face.

He saw the black fins of his pack slicing the Sea as they circled the prey which cowered on a rocking chunk of ice.

No! screamed Torak – but the Sea wolf's blood-hunger was a red tide engulfing his spirit.

And the prey was Wolf.

EIGHT

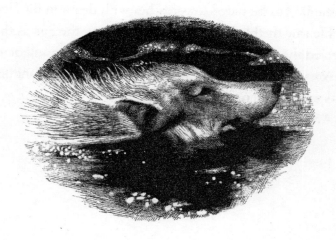

Wolf leapt into the Great Wet and floundered to the surface, waves smacking his muzzle, cold biting his chest. The wolves of the Wet were after him, their whistling and shrieking loud in his ears. Desperately he kept swimming, straining legs and paws and tail. *Where was the land?*

A giant wave lifted him and dashed him down. He was tumbling nose-over-tail through a blinding torrent of bubbles, he couldn't breathe, didn't know which way was up.

Dimly through the murk he made out huge blotchy shapes coming at him with lethal purpose. Far above, he saw the wavering glare of the Hot Bright Eye. He scrambled towards it with bursting chest.

As he struggled higher he heard new howls approaching with dizzying speed. These were not the howls of hunting wolves, they were deeper and slower, and the creatures who uttered them had vastly more power than the wolves of the Wet – they were *mountainfish*!

Wolf burst from the surface, panting and snapping air. He caught a jolting glimpse of tall black fins cutting the waves. The wolves of the Wet were nearly upon him, but behind them reared the mountainfish – and hope surged, for Wolf sensed from their booming howls that they weren't after him…

That maybe they were *helping* him?

Beating the Sea with his tail, Torak raced to overtake his pack-mates. He had to reach Wolf before they did.

Wolf looked pathetically small, his muzzle jutting above the waves, his paws bravely paddling as he swam towards a blur of land hopelessly far away.

Torak was frantic to defend him, but the Sea wolf's spirit was too strong, its blood-hunger too fierce, he couldn't turn it from the hunt. He was a wolf hunting Wolf, and his thunderous heart was ablaze with the ruthless urge to kill.

Stealthily he dived, then flipped over and rose towards the tiny creature thrashing against the glare. Speeding closer, he opened his jaws…

No! roared Torak. Yanking the great head aside, he snapped its jaws shut. The startled Sea wolf swivelled round to resume the attack, but Torak turned its movement into a playful head-butt which sent Wolf flying out of the water. He splashed down with a yelp, and again the Sea wolves went after him. They were too many, Torak couldn't hold them off.

But suddenly their eager squeals turned to alarm. A threat was rising towards them from the deep. Torak sensed it too, and in a flurry of clicks he 'saw' a pod of humpback whales making straight for his pack.

They were whales as he'd never seen them before, underwater creatures of lightness and grace, wielding their enormous flippers like wings, each thrust of their massive tails bringing them closer.

The Sea wolves were astonished: whales never attacked *them!* And yet these were, one whale swinging its flipper and sideswiping Torak's sister, sending her fleeing into the murk, another whale charging Torak. With a twist of his tail he dodged and swam to safety.

Through a wall of bubbles he saw that the great whales had surrounded Wolf, gliding around and beneath him so that the Sea wolves couldn't risk renewing their attack. The whales were *protecting* Wolf, like musk-oxen defending their young.

And now the Sea wolf's mother was calling off the hunt: the pack was leaving.

Torak hung back and poked his head out of the Sea.

Naiginn had been keeping a wary distance from the whales, and in the commotion he hadn't spotted Wolf – but he had seen Renn. Paddling with lightning speed, he was flying over the waves while she, grimacing with the pain of her injured hand, was desperately making for an islet that reared out of the water.

As Naiginn got within range of her, he flung down his paddle and seized his harpoon. Torak's spirit rose to protect his mate, and before the Sea wolf could resist, he was racing after the ice demon.

Renn had realized that she couldn't outrun Naiginn, and had grabbed Torak's bow. Baring her teeth in agony, she was trying to nock an arrow.

With a shout of triumph Naiginn drew back his arm to shoot. The wind was in his favour, and a harpoon has three times an arrow's range.

But suddenly Naiginn froze. He'd seen the Sea wolf blowing quick and hard as it bore down on him. For a heartbeat Torak saw the ice-blue eyes widen in the scarred face. Then Naiginn drew back his arm and cast the harpoon, and Torak, raising his tail to side-swipe the skinboat, felt a sting in one fluke. It put him off his stroke and he struck the Sea instead, washing his quarry overboard.

Once again Torak dived deep, then flipped round to rush his prey from beneath. He could see Naiginn floundering in the water, he could *not* escape.

And yet astonishingly, that was what he was doing. To Torak's fury, Naiginn was swimming towards his skinboat with long sure strokes – and something was wrong with Torak's tail, a numbness, he couldn't move his flukes...

He felt dizzy. The numbness was spreading to his belly, his flippers...

Wolfbane.

Naiginn had shot him with a poisoned harpoon.

NINE

Icy water smacked Torak in the face. He opened his eyes.

Renn put down the baler and bent over him. Her face was pale and drawn. She looked as if she was keeping a tight hold on her feelings.

'I can't move,' he mumbled.

'Your souls are still poisoned. It'll wear off.'

'Where's Naiginn?'

'Gone. Just before the fog closed in I saw him scramble back in his boat and make off. He didn't see me, he was too busy escaping the whales.'

Dizzy and sick, Torak struggled to sit up. 'I saw Wolf!

He was swimming towards an island, we have to reach him before Naiginn!'

'In this fog? It was all I could do to get us here.'

With a cry he struck the boat with his fist. The fog was so dense he couldn't see beyond the prow. He leant over the side and retched. Below him oarweed swirled and wavelets lapped rocks: that made him feel worse. 'Where are we?' he said.

'Some islet in the middle of nowhere. That island you saw – I saw it too, but it's a long way off.'

'How did we get here?'

'I paddled.' She sounded grim. 'After Naiginn shot that Sea wolf, the whales wouldn't let him near me. It was as if they'd been sent.' She threw him a glance, her face inscrutable. 'The Sea wolf he'd shot was floating on its side. It looked at me and I knew you were in its marrow. I thought it was going to drown and take you with it.'

'What happened to it?'

'Poison wore off, it swam away. Naiginn must've put just enough on the harpoon for a wolf, but not enough to affect a Sea wolf for long.' She paused, re-living it in her mind. 'By then the fog was so thick I couldn't see a thing. I found this cove by the sound of surf on rocks.'

He noticed that she was holding her injured hand to her chest. 'I didn't mean to hurt you,' he said.

'But you did.'

'I'm sorry.'

She ignored that. 'I know you're terrified of losing Wolf – but, Torak, I am your *mate*. Some day I may be the mother of our child.'

'Renn—'

'If you *ever* touch me in anger again, I will leave you and I will not come back!'

'I won't. I swear on my father's souls. That's one oath I'll never break.'

The canoe bumped against the rocks and she steadied it with the paddle. 'Not much daylight left. We need to get ashore and make camp.'

In fraught silence they carried the boat up the cove and overturned it on shoresticks. Torak woke a fire and left Renn feeding it driftwood. In a rock pool he found a big orange starfish and yanked handfuls of mussels off the rocks. Back at camp, he held the starfish's arms while Renn ate its salty innards. Then he prised open the mussels with a half-shell. He gave most of them to her.

She wasn't using her right hand, and he was shocked to see that her forearm was swollen, the thongs of her wrist-guard biting into her flesh. 'Let me loosen that for you—'

'Leave it.'

'Come on, Renn.' Gently he undid the knots and re-tied the thongs. He forced a smile. 'You have no bow, but you're still wearing a wrist-guard.'

'Fin-Kedinn gave it to me.'

Huddled by the fire, she looked small and easily hurt. That went through Torak like a knife. 'Renn ... I *had* to spirit walk in that Sea wolf! If I hadn't, I wouldn't have seen Wolf, or that island.'

She looked at him with glistening eyes. 'I know,' she said in a low voice. 'You'll do anything to find him. Even if it means leaving me behind.'

'No!'

'But that's what you did, Torak. You left me to save Wolf.'

Wolf had been swimming for ever. His eyes stung and his tail hurt. He could hardly feel his paws.

The wolves of the Wet had gone, and so had the mountainfish, but fog had swallowed the land. He had no idea where it was and he couldn't swim much further. He longed to shut his eyes and sleep...

A wave slapped him, jolting him awake. The Dark had come, and in the Up he saw the Bright White Eye and her many little cubs. What was that splashing?

Not far in front, he saw something strange: the head-branches of a stag jutting from the Wet. The stag was swimming steadily, it seemed to know where it was going. Wolf forced his legs to kick harder.

Fog swallowed the Up, and for an endless time Wolf followed the stag. At last the wind turned and he smelt *Forest!* He heard waves crashing on rocks. Now hills were looming in the fog – and to his elation he saw that they were not false hills of Bright Hard Cold, they were covered in trees!

The stag heaved itself onto the rocks and shook itself. Then it picked its way up the shore and disappeared into the Forest.

Waves lifted Wolf nearer the rocks, then sucked him back. Next time they did this he scrambled onto slippery mounds of salt-grass and lay panting, flanks heaving. He was safe!

Too weak to shake the Wet from his fur, he lurched to his feet – and nearly fell over. The land seemed to be rocking beneath his paws, as if the Great Wet still had him in her clutches.

Beyond mounds of crunchy salt-grass, he smelt rich rotten mud – and beyond that, Forest. Wolf smelt pine trees and moss and deer, wolverine and squirrel – but the scents were subtly different from those he knew, and with a pang he realized that this was not *his* Forest. It had no wolves. No Tall Tailless. No pack.

Wolf was too exhausted to go another step. Feeling horribly alone, he slumped onto the salt-grass and shut his eyes.

The Light came and the ravens who belonged to the pack flew down, cawing like wolf cubs. Wolf tried to thump his tail but it hurt too much.

The ravens were poking about in the mud. Now they were soaring with shells in their talons, and dropping them with a clatter onto the rocks. They did it over and over, and though some shells bounced, some shattered – and the ravens swooped and pecked the worms inside. *Clever* ravens!

Wolf staggered to the rocks and waited hopefully. He was too weak to steal many worms from the ravens, but he did get a couple, or maybe they let him. The worms were delicious, and hunger came roaring back.

Wolf ate some salt-grass, but it tasted bad so he spat it out. An odd little creature with big foreclaws scuttled past and he pounced. It gave him a painful nip on the nose and he let it go. Scrabbling in the salt-grass, he found more of the nasty nipping creatures, and clouds of biting midges.

An otter emerged from the Great Wet with a fish in her jaws. Casting Wolf a mocking glance, she scampered into the Forest with her prey.

Then in a rock pool he found an extremely strange creature with a squashy blob of a body and long snaky legs, like a giant spider. The creature saw him coming and turned pale, squirting clouds of black and squeezing itself into an impossibly small crack. Wolf clawed at it with his forepaw and managed to yank it out, but it wrapped itself around his muzzle. It was squidgy yet alarmingly strong, and Wolf staggered blindly, thrashing his head. Desperately he grabbed the creature between his forepaws and tugged, and it plopped into the pool and slithered into the crack.

Defeated, Wolf plodded miserably towards the trees. Mud sucked hungrily at his forepaws, and he reared on his hind legs. His forepaws sank deeper. Growling, he fought the mud, but it held him fast, sucking at his haunches, his belly.

Wolf was stuck. In this horrible place even *mud* was after him.

And now the Great Wet was creeping up the shore towards him.

TEN

'Are you hurt?' panted Torak as he helped Renn onto the rocks.

'I'm fine,' she gasped. 'But look at the canoe!'

They'd paddled within arrowshot of the island when they'd struck a raft of black ice. The boat lay in the surf like a wounded beast, a gaping hole in its hull.

Before them stretched a sandy black shore strewn with driftwood bleached silver by wind and sun. Behind it rose a dank wall of silent, moss-hung spruce. The Forest beyond could only be guessed at from spiky treetops floating in mist.

Sodden and shivering, they squelched through mounds of rotting kelp. In a rock pool Renn saw a green anemone as big as her head. It drew in its tentacles and gave her a baleful one-eyed stare: *The Sea Mother's had enough of you.*

Hurriedly they woke a fire and pulled off their wet clothes, warming up by scrubbing each other all over with handfuls of dryish seaweed. While Renn checked their gear, Torak turned their sleeping-sacks inside out and hung them to dry. Then, half-dressed, they rescued the stricken canoe, making it safe from the tides by wedging it behind driftwood at the edge of the trees.

While Torak was searching the shore for wolf tracks, Renn plucked beard-moss off the trees and made a poultice for her hand. The scab had cracked open and it hurt worse than ever. The swelling was worse too, and she was beginning to worry about the blackening sickness. What if she lost her hand and could never shoot again...

Behind her the Forest was utterly still. A branch fell with a muffled thump, emphasizing the silence. From beyond the clouds came an eagle's lonely cry.

Torak returned. 'Nothing,' he said in disgust.

'Maybe the tide washed away his tracks.'

'Maybe. If he is here, he'll be in the Forest.' He cupped his hands to his mouth to howl – then thought better of it.

'You're right,' Renn said quietly. 'Naiginn could be here too.'

An eagle swooped and plucked a fish from the bay, then flew to its nest high in a spruce.

'Which island d'you think this is?' said Torak.

'Definitely not Seal Island.'

'Not Cormorant, either. Kelp? Didn't Apsu say it's covered in trees?'

She nodded. She only knew three members of the Kelp Clan, and those not well. Halut and her brothers had been on a trading mission when the Thunderstar struck, and the Ravens had taken them in: but the Kelps hadn't mixed much with the other survivors. Renn wished now that she'd got to know them better.

'All I know about Kelps,' said Torak, 'is that they think wolves are sacred, so they try to look like them. And there aren't any wolves on their island.'

'So if Wolf is here, they'll know it.'

'Thing is, Apsu said they camp in the east, as it's more sheltered. And I'm pretty sure we're in the west.'

'Well, before we do anything,' said Renn, 'I need food and water, I'm *really* thirsty!'

The bay had no fresh water and they'd lost their waterskins overboard, but Torak still had the small seal-gut one he wore under his jerkin; they drank what was in it, then packed it with drift ice, to melt. After that they had a swift yet strengthening daymeal of giant scallops, bashing them open with rocks and munching the sweet, tender flesh raw.

It was past noon by the time they were fully dressed. Shouldering their packs and sleeping-sacks, they headed into the Forest.

With that first step, the voice of the Sea fell away and they found themselves breathing the earthy tang they'd known all their lives.

'I've missed this,' murmured Torak.

'Me too,' said Renn.

It was much warmer in the Forest, only the odd patch of snow, and very quiet and very green. Moss muffled their footsteps and dripped from every bough, a green tide smothering logs, stumps, roots. Their boots sank ankle-deep.

If it was the mossiest Forest they'd ever been in, it was also the densest and most tangled. Branches snagged their gear and tugged at their hair, making every step a struggle, and in no time they were covered in mud and spruce needles. Brambles concealed boggy pools, moss cloaked fissures between roots: Torak sank to his knee in one and nearly broke his shin. Moss also made rotten wood appear sound: Renn grabbed a branch to steady herself and it crumbled, pitching her backwards onto Torak.

And yet they sensed no ill will from the Forest; only a stubborn resistance to their venturing further.

'It doesn't feel *unfriendly*,' Torak said in bemusement. 'It's just – I don't think these trees know people. I wouldn't want to chop one down to mend the canoe.'

As he said it the surrounding trees shivered in a breeze, showering them with droplets. 'I said I *wouldn't*!' he told them quickly.

Unable to see the sky, they soon lost their bearings and were reduced to taking whatever way they could. They had the uneasy sense that the Forest was making sure that they only went where it wanted them to go.

Apart from a few fat yellow slugs, they saw neither hunters nor prey, although the mossy Forest floor was littered with mussel shells, fish bones and half-eaten wings – dropped by eagles and ravens, or left by otters and wolverines.

Renn found a neat pile of droppings by a flattened patch of moss where a deer had made its bed. Torak spotted claw-marks on a tree-trunk, and beneath it, in a pool of black mud, a single paw-print: the pine marten had leant down and tested the mud with one paw, then decided not to risk it and fled back up the tree.

'But no sign of Wolf,' Torak said with a scowl.

'D'you have *any* idea where we're going?' Renn said crossly. 'Because I don't!'

He shook his head. 'But I think the trees want us to go that way.'

Wearily she struggled after him. She felt naked without her bow; and though she'd whistled for Rip and Rek they hadn't come.

An eggshell crunched beneath her boot, and with a pang she realized that it wasn't long till Egg Dawn, when the World Spirit turns from a woman with red willow-branch hair to a man with the antlers of a stag. Renn liked Egg Dawn. The clans had feasts, and Mages collected crossbill eggs and—

'There's a clearing ahead!' cried Torak, pushing eagerly forwards. 'I think I can see... Oh.' His shoulders slumped.

'What is it?'

'Come and see,' he said in a flat voice.

Renn pushed through to him. 'Oh no, it can't be!' she exclaimed.

They had reached the edge of the Forest. Before them stretched a sandy black shore littered with driftwood, and below it rocks and the softly lapping Sea.

And at their feet, exactly where they'd wedged it behind driftwood, lay their canoe.

Darkfur wants Wolf to play with her. Whining softly, she is snuffle-licking his muzzle and soft-biting his ears: *Come on, get up!* Wolf is lying on his belly, breathing her wonderful warm smell and her meaty breath. He *wants* to get up but he's too tired. He's too weak even to thump his tail.

The ravens were calling: Quork! Quork! *Follow!*

Wolf opened his eyes. Darkfur was gone. He was stuck in the cold mud, only his head and shoulders poking out. The Great Wet was stealing ever closer.

But Wolf was no longer alone. The ravens that belonged to the pack were flying overhead, and a small half-grown tailless was sprawled on her belly, trying to dig him out. She had a good strong fishy smell and a squashed-looking face with impressively sharp teeth, for a tailless; but though she was very determined, the mud was winning. Soon it would swallow Wolf. He was too spent to fight.

When he woke again, the female had brought help: three sturdy male taillesses were hard at work digging. They were full-growns and clever, lying on their bellies on matted salt-grass so that the mud couldn't swallow them. One reached in and grabbed Wolf's foreleg, yanked it free, placed the caked paw on the salt-grass. Next they freed the other foreleg. Now they were hauling at his hindquarters: Wolf yelped when they touched his tail. After that things went fuzzy.

He woke to find himself lying in soft, dry moss. He was beautifully warm and *clean*, not a speck of mud on his fur. He smelt that the taillesses had brought him to their great fish-smelling Den, and that it lay between the Forest and the Great Wet, who was no longer after him, but murmuring peacefully many bounds away.

The same three male taillesses who had rescued Wolf appeared with the half-grown female, who was carrying herrings in her forepaws. One of the males spoke sharply to her and tried to take the fish, but Wolf growled at him: *Leave her alone!* Chastened, the male stepped back.

The little female approached at a respectful crouch and set the herrings near Wolf's muzzle. Wolf was too weak even to move his head. Far too weak to eat.

Well, maybe a bite.

Three herrings later, he felt well enough to lift his head.

The female brought a large, blotchy, quivering blob that smelt strongly of the Great Wet. It was a giant spider like the one which had clamped onto Wolf's muzzle, but this one was Not-Breath, so he nibbled a snaky leg. It was deliciously chewy and it had no bones. Wolf gobbled the lot.

As he was drifting off again, he felt small furless forepaws shyly stroking his flank. His tail hurt too much to thump, so instead he thanked the half-grown tailless by sleeking back his ears.

Lights and Darks went by, and gradually Wolf grew strong enough to pad about between naps.

The little female gave him Wet to drink in a hollow stone, and squidgy giant spiders. The fish-smelling taillesses had made him a comfortable sleeping-spot not far from their Den, and had thoughtfully planted a wall of saplings to keep their dogs from pestering him. They even put out fish for the ravens who belonged to the pack; the birds had grown almost too fat to fly.

From time to time, many taillesses would come and stand behind the saplings and gaze at Wolf over the top. Like the little female, they had fangs and squashed faces, and a rich fishy smell. They were friendly and respectful, but Wolf sensed that they wanted something from him. He didn't know what.

At last Wolf knew that he was strong enough to go hunting in the Forest. He was disconcerted to find more saplings barring his way. They were too high to jump and he couldn't find any gaps, not even when he trotted all the way around.

Alarmed, he circled them again. No gaps. He scrabbled with his forepaws to dig his way out. The saplings went too deep, he couldn't get under.

It crashed upon Wolf that he was trapped. The taillesses had caught him as surely as if they'd enticed him into a pit.

He raised his muzzle to howl. He shut it again. Why howl, when there were no wolves to hear?

The little half-grown female was peering down at him from behind the saplings, and Wolf sensed that she felt sorry for him. She dropped a herring into his pen. He ignored it.

Why eat, when he would never see Tall Tailless and his pack again?

ELEVEN

The crunch of Dark's snowshoes was loud in the stillness as he climbed towards the Den. He'd promised Torak that he would keep an eye on Darkfur, and he needed to see the wolves for his own sake too. They had helped him in the past. Maybe they could help him find the Walker, the mad old wanderer who had once been a Mage, and whose shattered mind still held kernels of wisdom.

Ark flew from pine to pine, showering Dark with snow. Brushing himself off, he watched her thoughtfully. The white raven had learnt that trick from Rip and Rek. Was she trying to tell him something? Or simply being playful?

To his dismay, the Den was deserted. He guessed that Darkfur was higher up the ridge, working on the spare Den she'd been digging in case this one collapsed.

A thin cold wind hissed over the scattered droppings and well-chewed bones. Dark sat on a rock by the Den's entrance and put his elbows on his knees. A wave of dejection washed over him.

It was days since he and Kujai had done the charm, and he had no idea if it had worked – or if Torak and Renn were still alive. That morning he'd woken with a gnawing sense that there was something else he had to do, something important. And on top of everything, Fin-Kedinn needed him to find the Walker. At the Raven Leader's direction, Dark had left pebbles bearing Fin-Kedinn's mark at several of the Walker's old haunts. But again, that was days ago – and so far, nothing.

It's too much, Dark thought bleakly, staring at the dirty snow between his boots. I can't do it.

That was when he saw it: the faint print of a foot. His heart began to pound. The print was peculiarly blunt. The Walker had lost his toes to frostbite. And even in winter he wore no boots.

Dark wasn't much good at tracking and the snow had been trampled by many paws, but a few paces from the Den he found another print. Definitely the Walker.

Pebble appeared above the Den.

'Pebble, it's me!' Dark said, keeping his voice quiet and reassuring.

The young wolf hesitated – then sleeked back his ears and trotted down the slope. Always nervous, he was even more on edge now: the loss of Wolf and Whitethroat had hit him hard.

'I need to find the Walker,' Dark told him, stooping to scratch his furry flank. He pointed at the footprint. 'You like the old man. D'you know where he went?'

Eagerly Pebble sniffed the print. He glanced at Dark and gave a tentative twitch of his tail, uncertain how to help.

'No, of course you don't,' Dark said sadly. 'It's just... Oh, Pebble. Fin-Kedinn needs me to find the Walker, he needs the Walker to heal his leg – because I can't! I'm a Mage, but I don't know what to do, I've tried everything—' He broke off, alarmed by the anguish in his voice.

The young wolf's amber gaze grazed his, then slid politely away. Ark lit onto Dark's shoulder, blinking and gurgling to tell him she was sorry. They knew he was worried, but they couldn't understand why. For that he needed a human friend.

As he was leaving he felt the tightness in his chest which told him a demon had been here. He sensed it was a lesser demon – there had been lots in the Forest since the Thunderstar – and that it wasn't here now; but he ran back and dabbed earthblood above the Den's entrance, to protect Darkfur when she returned. Again he had that nagging feeling that he was missing something.

He searched the valley all day but found no more tracks, and around mid-afternoon he came upon a Willow

Clan boy and a Viper girl checking their snares. At least, that's what they said they were doing, but really they just wanted to be together; they kept grinning and nudging each other, and barely heard what Dark said.

'Are you sure you haven't seen him, or heard tell of him?' he said impatiently. 'A one-eyed outcast? Used to be Otter Clan?'

The boy shook his head without bothering to conceal his lack of interest, but the girl said vaguely that her fa might have seen someone like that.

'When? Where?' cried Dark.

'Um – sorry, can't remember.'

The boy was tugging her wrist. 'Come on, let's go!'

'Sorry!' Smiling helplessly, she let the boy pull her away.

Watching them go, Dark's spirits plunged. They made him feel left out; sometimes Torak and Renn did too, though they didn't mean to. And soon it'll be spring, he thought savagely. Everything in the Forest pairing off – except me.

The setting sun was lighting the clouds from beneath, like the embers of a giant fire. As he watched, the glow died and the clouds turned to ash. He found himself thinking about Kujai. They'd been fishing twice, but the last time the Sea-eagle boy hadn't stopped complaining about his wretched canoe, and Dark had snapped at him and they'd fought. The bruise on his jaw was a painful reminder. He hadn't seen Kujai since.

Stupid, he thought angrily. Why not just go and see him and sort it out?

Well, because he hasn't been to see you, so clearly he doesn't want to.

The first stars were trembling in the sky by the time he reached camp. The dogs were curled up in the snow, and smoke was rising from the roof-hole of the great log shelter which in winter housed the entire Raven Clan.

Fin-Kedinn wasn't inside, and someone told Dark that he was in the smaller shelter at the edge of camp which they kept for people with fever. 'He isn't sick,' they assured him. 'He just wanted to talk to the Walker alone.'

'*The Walker?*' cried Dark.

Fin-Kedinn appeared in the doorway. 'Ah, Dark, you're back. Come with me.'

'How did you find him?' said Dark, slowing his pace to match Fin-Kedinn's limp.

'I didn't,' said the Raven Leader. 'He found one of the pebbles you left. Shambled into camp just after dusk.'

'What does he say about your leg? Can he help?'

'He won't say anything, he's pretending he doesn't understand. I thought you could talk to him, Mage to Mage.'

'Mm,' Dark said doubtfully. The Walker had never treated him with anything but scorn.

The fever hut was a typical three-sided Raven shelter with a reindeer-hide roof and no front wall, just a crossbeam which deflected smoke from the fire while trapping the heat inside; even on frosty nights you only needed a sleeping-sack to stay snug.

But if Fin-Kedinn had hoped to entice the Walker into the warmth, the old man was having none of it. He squatted in the snow beyond the fire, skinning a hare. Fin-Kedinn's one-eared dog, Grip, stood beside him, appreciatively sniffing his stench.

The old man didn't raise his head at their approach, but he cackled at Grip. 'Look, dog, he's brought Chalk Boy!'

With his knotted limbs and twiggy mane and beard, the Walker resembled an ancient storm-battered tree. Despite the cold he wore nothing but a few rotten hides which he'd ripped from carcasses without bothering to clean: a mouldy deerskin about his loins, foot-bindings of stinking eel hide, and a grimy reindeer pelt for a cape. He'd knotted the forelegs around his neck; when he moved, the hooves bumped against his chest.

Fin-Kedinn seated himself in the shelter with his bad leg stiffly before him and resumed work on a net which hung from the cross-beam. 'I thought you could talk to Dark,' he told the Walker, knotting kelp twine at the edge of the net.

'Mages!' The Walker spat a gob of green snot that landed on Dark's boot. 'What good are they?'

'I need your help,' said Dark. 'Fin-Kedinn's wound *appears* healed – clean scar, no blackening sickness – but something's wrong inside.' He listed the medicines and charms which he and Renn had tried. 'Nothing works,' he said.

Ark flew onto the old man's bony shoulder and pecked a louse from his beard. He gave her a toothless black grin and stroked her snowy wing. 'The Walker was a Mage once,' he crooned to her.

'We know,' said Fin-Kedinn with an edge to his voice.

'Till he lost his eye,' the old man told the bird. 'Popped right out and a raven ate it. Ha! Ravens like eyes.'

Fin-Kedinn's jaw tightened as he checked the size of the mesh with a bone net gauge.

'The pain never lets up,' explained Dark.

'So?' snapped the Walker. 'Everyone's in pain!'

'It's getting worse,' growled Fin-Kedinn.

The old man clawed open the hare's belly. 'What's he think the Walker can do?' he mumbled through a mouthful of bloody guts.

'You've helped us before,' said Dark.

'Nets! Nets!' muttered the old man. 'Are they trying to *trap* the Walker?'

'Of course not,' said Fin-Kedinn. 'Although you can have this shelter for a long as you like, and the sleeping-sack.'

The Walker writhed, as if the thought of comfort hurt.

The Raven Leader stopped working and fixed him with his vivid blue gaze. 'I'm asking you for help. Not for my clan, but for me. We used to be friends.'

The ruined face contorted with rage. 'That's not *fair!*' he shrieked. Flinging the hare into the snow, he leapt into the shelter and tore aside the net. 'Show the Walker! Show!'

At close quarters his stench was overpowering: Dark fought the urge to retch. Apprehensively he watched Fin-Kedinn untie his belt and ease his legging down his hip.

The great puckered scar ran the length of his thigh. His face remained impassive as the Walker probed the scar with one grimy claw. 'A demon did this,' said the old man.

'The demon bear,' said Fin-Kedinn sharply. 'Don't pretend you don't know.'

With a snicker the Walker sat back on his haunches. 'The Walker hunts demons in caves, not bodies. This demon bit deep.'

'What does that mean?' Fin-Kedinn said between his teeth.

'It's eating the marrow. Soon you won't be able to walk.'

The fire crackled and spat. Grip stood at the mouth of the shelter, anxiously watching his master's face.

Slowly, Fin-Kedinn re-tied his belt. His hand went to the small yewwood raven on the thong at his throat. 'You're sure there is no cure?'

The Walker cackled. 'Oh, there's a cure! It'll end the pain for ever! It's called death!' Still cackling, he snatched the mangled hare and disappeared into the night.

Ark flew after him. Dark didn't take his eyes from Fin-Kedinn.

For a long time the Raven Leader stared into the flames. His expression never altered, but Dark sensed the turmoil within.

Slowly, Fin-Kedinn picked up the net gauge. He re-hung the net from its hook. He squared his shoulders. 'Well, that's that,' he said quietly. And went back to work.

Half-blinded by tears, Dark blundered after the Walker. Anger and pain were churning inside him – and shame: because he was powerless to help the man he'd come to love as a father.

Spotting the Walker among the birches, he shouted at him to stop.

'What now?' snapped the old man.

'There must be something you can do!'

The Walker can't help! Nobody can!'

'Wait!'

The Walker turned on him. '*Always* Chalk Boy misses the point! Why's he whining about Fin-Kedinn? He should be thinking what's coming next!'

'What do you mean?'

The old man spat scornfully. 'What's he think he's doing, banishing the *little* demons, the slitherers and scurriers? That's not going to help when the great one comes!'

'You mean – Naiginn?'

The deep eye glinted in the ruined face. 'Magecraft's like carving. You've got to think ahead!'

Suddenly Dark realized what he'd been missing. 'Even if he's killed,' he murmured. 'What happens to his souls?'

The Walker bared his foetid stumps in a grin. 'At last Chalk Boy's starting to *think*! An ice demon's spirit loose in the Forest! Wouldn't take it long to find another host.'

'How do I stop it?'

'Why ask the Walker? Chalk Boy already knows!'

'No, I don't, that's why I'm asking you!'

'Is Chalk Boy a Mage or a mouse?' roared the old man. 'Does he think the Walker will *always* be here to help?'

'No, but—'

'Is Chalk Boy *blind*?' A sweep of his scrawny arm took in the frosty birch trees and the fever hut in its orange shell of firelight. 'Can't he *see* what's right under his nose?' Snarling, he shambled into the night.

Soon afterwards Dark heard his voice on the wind: 'The answer's in front of him if he has eyes to see!'

TWELVE

Fin-Kedinn was still working on his net when Dark got
back.

In the firelight the Raven Leader's face was calm, only the
lines at the sides of his mouth showed that he was in pain.
Beside him lay his axe, knife and fishing spear, along with
a pile of evenly sized pebbles he was tying on as weights.

Everything so orderly, thought Dark in disbelief. After
what he's just heard.

'Ah, there you are,' said the Raven Leader. 'What he said
about my leg – we'll keep it to ourselves, yes?'

Dark crawled into the shelter and sat on the reindeer
pelts, hugging his knees. 'Why did you want me here
when he told you?'

'You're my Mage, you need to know.'

'Is that the only reason?'

The blue eyes met his. 'From time to time, Dark, a flock of geese changes its leader. The old bird slips behind and a younger one takes its place.'

Dark stared at him in horror. 'But you're not old!'

'Doesn't matter. When I can no longer walk, I won't be able to lead the clan.'

'*No!*'

'Dark, it's allright,' Fin-Kedinn said gently. 'I wanted to hear the truth, and I have.'

Dark turned and stared at the night sky. The half-eaten moon shone palely. The First Tree was a faint shimmering green, infinitely remote.

'You know,' said Fin-Kedinn. 'I never expected to be Leader. Everyone thought my older brother – Renn's father – would be chosen instead. I didn't *want* to be Leader. Didn't think I could do it.'

Dark was incredulous. '*You?*'

Fin-Kedinn looked amused. 'Me.' Cutting a length of kelp twine, he tied it crossways around a pebble. 'So tell me,' he said in a different tone. 'Just now when you went after the Walker, did you learn anything I need to hear?'

Briefly, Dark told him what the old man had said about the ice demon's souls. 'We have to banish them to the Otherworld. If we don't, he might find a new host and the whole thing starts again.'

'Can it be done?'

'I don't know, I don't know the right charm. I wish Renn was here.'

'So do I. Have you any idea what's happened to them?'

Unhappily, Dark shook his head.

'I miss them,' Fin-Kedinn said in an undertone. 'I want to see them again.'

'Me too.' Picking up Fin-Kedinn's knife, he turned it in his fingers. It was made of red deer antler, the haft wound with sinew for a sure grip, the blade fitted with sharp flakes of dark-grey flint. Like everything the Raven Leader made, it was simple yet highly effective.

'I think,' said Dark, running his finger over the flints, 'I have to be the one to kill Naiginn.'

'No, Dark. You're not a killer.'

'If Torak or Renn do it they'll be outcast. And my father—'

'—was in league with Naiginn, so you want to atone. I tell you again, you are not a killer of men.'

A log settled on the fire, sending a flurry of sparks into the night. In the Forest a tree creaked.

Dark watched Fin-Kedinn tie the pebble to the edge of the net. In his mind he heard the Walker's unfeeling cackle: *Oh, there's a cure! It's called death!*

'Do you fear death?' Dark asked in a low voice.

Fin-Kedinn paused in his work. 'Dying, yes – if it hurts. But not death. I think it's like a strong wind blowing away footprints in the snow.'

Dark's eyes stung.

Fin-Kedinn cut another piece of twine and chose another pebble. 'That Sea-eagle boy,' he said briskly. 'Have you two been fishing again?'

'Um – no. Not for a few days.'

'Why not?'

'We had a fight.'

'Ah. I wondered.' He indicated the bruise on Dark's jaw. 'What was it about?'

'Oh, he kept saying how much he missed his canoe, so I said it's only a boat, and that did it.'

Fin-Kedinn chuckled. 'So make up! Kujai's clever and kind. A good young man.'

'I know.' With a scowl Dark plucked at the reindeer pelt. He thought how different the Sea-eagles were from his own clan, the Swans. 'Why do some clans get things so *wrong?*' he muttered.

'What d'you mean?'

'If Kujai's father had been born a Swan like me, they'd have abandoned him in the Mountains just because he doesn't look like everyone else.'

'That's what people did in the old times. Some clans haven't changed since then, some have.'

Dark looked at him. 'It was a pretty big change when you made me Mage.'

'It was,' agreed the Raven Leader. 'No one's ever had a Mage from a different clan. I'm proud of that.'

'Have you ever regretted it?'

'Not for a heartbeat.' He paused. 'You'd make a good Leader too.'

'*Me?* Pff!'

'You took charge after the Thunderstar struck.'

'For less than a day.'

'But you did it well.' He unhooked the net from the cross-beam and rolled it up. 'I think I'll sleep here tonight. Tell the others, will you? And, Dark...'

'Yes?'

'That charm to banish the ice demon's souls. You'll find a way.'

Dark flushed. Fin-Kedinn wouldn't have said that if he didn't believe it was true.

Before he left, he dragged another log onto the fire. Fin-Kedinn had stowed his net and his weapons at the back of the shelter, and was unrolling his sleeping-sack.

The answer's in front of him, the Walker had said. *If he has eyes to see.*

And suddenly, as neatly as a flint flake slotting into the groove of a knife, Dark saw the answer, and knew what he had to do.

He waited till noon, and when there was still no sign of Kujai he swallowed his pride and trudged along the frozen river to the Sea-eagles' camp.

Kujai was busy in his boat shed and didn't notice Dark, but his dog gave him a drop-eared welcome. Ark settled in a tree, preening her tail feathers and keeping a wary eye on the dog.

Kujai sat on a log by the fire, whittling a piece of elk bone. His head was bent: all Dark could see was his shaggy fair hair, and the four-clawed mark of the Sea-eagle on the back of his hand. He had good hands, square and strong. Like Dark's they were covered in little nicks; that happened when you did lots of carving.

Sensing he wasn't alone, Kujai raised his head and gave Dark a long, steady look. His eyes were the grey-blue of the Sea on a cloudy day, and dizzyingly deep.

A little shakily, Dark hunkered down on the other side of the fire. Kujai resumed his whittling. Dark noticed a purple bruise on his cheekbone, overlying his birthmark. 'Did I do that?' he said.

'Yes,' Kujai said evenly.

'Does it hurt?'

'A bit.' He glanced at Dark's jaw. 'Does that?'

'A bit.'

Kujai grunted.

'Sorry I said that about your boat,' muttered Dark.

Kujai stopped carving. 'I shouldn't have got so cross. It's just that my big brothers always told me I'd never make a good canoe, so when I finally managed it...' He shrugged, and resumed carving. Now and then he scooped a handful of what looked like wood shavings from a bowl at his feet and crammed them in his mouth. He nodded at Dark to help himself.

'What is it?' said Dark.

'Toasted sea-wrack,' mumbled Kujai.

The sea-wrack was crunchy and popped saltily on Dark's tongue. He took another handful and they munched in silence.

'You know,' said Kujai, 'you're better at fighting than you look.'

'Thanks,' Dark said drily.

'Torak did warn me.'

'Torak?'

'Before he left he took me aside. *Listen*, he said. *Just because he's gentle doesn't mean he's weak!* Kujai picked a shred of sea-wrack from between his front teeth. 'He said your fa abandoned you when you were eight, and you lived by yourself in the Mountains for seven winters.'

Dark felt the heat rising to his face. He found himself telling Kujai about the little stone creatures he'd carved to keep him company in his cave, one for each moon; and how he used to talk to them, and how bad he'd felt when he'd had to leave most of them behind. He'd never told anyone that, not even Torak or Renn. He wondered how it was possible that in less than half a moon this Sea-eagle boy should have become so familiar to him – and so necessary.

'It's not true that you were born without colour,' Kujai remarked. 'Your eyes are pale grey and your eyelids are pink, like anyone else's. And that bruise I gave you is every colour of the rainbow.'

Dark laughed. 'What's that you're making?'

'Fishing spear. A *Sea-eagle* spear. D'you know how it works?'

'No. But I'm pretty sure you're going to tell me.'

It was Kujai's turn to laugh. 'If you catch a big fish with an ordinary spear and the fish thrashes hard enough, it might snap the shaft – and you lose your catch. But *we* make our spearheads *separately*. We cut a socket in it like this, so it fits onto the shaft. Then we tie a length of strong twine around the head *and* the shaft, so that they can't get separated. That way if your fish wrenches the head off the shaft, the twine keeps them attached – so you catch your fish without snapping your spear.'

'Clever,' said Dark.

Kujai put down the spearhead and pushed the hair out of his face. 'So what was it you came for?'

'You mean, apart from saying sorry?'

'Apart from saying sorry.'

Dark took the spearhead and turned it in his fingers. 'There's a charm I have to do. Not now, but soon, I think. I need your help.'

'Allright.'

That took Dark's breath away. Kujai hadn't asked what the charm was for, or what it involved, he'd simply said yes.

'I need to make a spear,' said Dark, handing back the head. 'And I need to make a net.'

THIRTEEN

'What are we doing wrong?' muttered Torak for the tenth time.

'I don't know,' Renn said wearily. She was tired and dispirited. All she could think about was the pain in her arm.

It was dawn on the fourth day since they'd reached Kelp Island, and yesterday their third attempt at finding a way through the Forest had ended in failure. She'd made offerings of smoked herring and called on her clan guardians for help. Torak had left waymarkers as they went, so that they'd know if they'd been there before. But always the trees led them quietly back to where they'd started.

'I think we should try trekking along the coast,' said Torak. 'Then we *can't* get lost. And we're bound to come to a river, and Wolf's more likely to be near water.'

'Fine.' Heaving herself to her feet, Renn shouldered her pack. Her arm was swollen to the elbow. She pictured worms of sickness burrowing into her marrow.

The tide was out and the sand firm underfoot, so at first they made good progress. The shore was busy with oystercatchers pecking clams; eagles and gulls squabbling over crabs, and agile little turnstones racing up and down to avoid the waves. Torak walked slowly with his head bent, seeking signs of Wolf. Renn trudged after him, staring at her feet.

By mid-afternoon the pain was so bad she was walking in a nightmare. Sleety rain stung her face, and although she was chilled to the bone, she realized with a shock that she was sweating under her clothes. Oh no, she thought. Not fever!

They came to a rocky shore where the Forest overhung the Sea, forcing them to scramble over fallen trunks and stumps. Torak paused to pluck mussels from the rocks and offered some to her, but she shook her head. 'Not hungry.'

'That's not like you. Your arm's worse, isn't it?'

A convulsive shiver gripped her. 'I'm a Mage – but I can't heal myself.'

'We have to get you out of this sleet. Here, I'll carry your gear.'

He tucked her axe in his belt, took her sleeping-sack and strapped it to his back. That only left her with her slingshot, medicine pouch and the pouch of smoked herrings, but it still felt too much.

'Just a bit further,' said Torak. 'We'll find shelter.'

But where? No shore remained, only slimy rocks below looming cliffs, with the Sea not two paces away drenching them in spray. Renn would have fallen if Torak hadn't put his arm round her waist to steady her.

'There's a cave up ahead,' he said in her ear.

She made out a deep cleft in the cliff, like a giant axe-cut. A heavy swell was surging in and out. She didn't like the look of it, but they had no choice.

Inside, the cleft was so narrow that Torak could touch both sides with his outstretched arms. Dank walls echoed with the soughing of the Sea. The salt smell was overpowering.

Moonlight slanted in from high above, revealing an overhang at the back that offered scant shelter. It was piled with driftwood and kelp: Torak made a nest for Renn and helped her into her sleeping-sack, wrapping his own around her shoulders.

'What about you?' she said through chattering teeth.

'I'll wake a fire, soon get you warm.'

Blearily she watched him set to work with tinder and strike-fire. The wood was damp, but at last flames leapt, lighting the strong bony planes of his face. Renn was startled to find herself blinking back tears.

'Now I know you're ill,' he said. 'You never cry.'

'I d-do sometimes,' she stuttered.

'Name one time in the past two summers.'

He was trying to keep her talking, to take her mind off the pain. She attempted a smile, but only managed a grimace.

The fire crackled, sending smoke twisting towards the stars. Slipping off her gauntlets, Renn tried to warm her hands. She wondered if Wolf was here on the island – or were fishes nibbling his corpse? And what about Naiginn? The ice demon's face rose before her. She hated that he'd slipped into her head.

'D'you think Naiginn's here?' said Torak as if he'd heard her thoughts.

'I haven't s-sensed him… But yes, I do.'

He fed the fire more wood. 'Something I can't work out. If I did kill him—'

'Oh, Torak, no—'

'But if I did. What happens to his souls?'

She blinked. 'I hadn't thought of that. He's a demon. Killing won't be enough. We'd have to banish his spirit to the Otherworld.'

'How?'

'I don't know, I—' She was gripped by another convulsive shudder. 'C-can't believe I didn't think of it…' A wave of nausea washed over her and she shut her eyes. The noise of the swell was suddenly louder, the Sea smell overwhelming.

Torak rose to his feet. 'We need to climb higher.'

'What? Why? I'm staying here.'

Gently he took his sleeping-sack from her shoulders and pulled her to her feet. 'Renn, I'm sorry. This cave was a bad idea.'

'But I'm too sick to climb!'

'I'm afraid you have to. We can't stay here, the tide's coming in.'

Torak found another handhold and hoisted himself higher. He'd spotted a ledge halfway up the cleft. If he could get Renn onto that, she'd be safe from the Sea, and he might be able to climb all the way to the top, and find something for making rope and haul her out...

Below him she stood swaying and blinking in the smoke. With each surge the waves were crashing closer. Soon they'd be over her boots.

'Climb to me!' he shouted. 'It's not far, you can do it!'

She tried, but fell back with a yelp. She couldn't pull herself up with only one hand.

'I'll help you!' he panted, scrambling back to her. She was shivering uncontrollably, but he managed to steady her while he climbed alongside, and they made it a little higher.

Below them the Sea came rushing in, quenching the fire and sending smoke billowing around them. Torak stared at the water foaming where they'd been standing moments before. In the crashing of the waves he seemed to hear the Sea Mother's cavernous laughter: *Did you think I'd finished with you?*

He felt a wild urge to yell: *Why are you punishing us? What did we do wrong?* But he already knew the answer. They hadn't done anything wrong – and the Sea Mother didn't care.

Renn was pressing herself against the rocks. Her lips were blue in a face as white as bone.

'Hold on,' he told her. 'I'll find a way to the ledge, then come back and help you... Renn? Did you hear me?'

She nodded, but she kept widening her eyes as if she was having trouble keeping them open.

Desperation lent Torak skill and he found a way to the ledge. As he scrambled onto it he touched something leathery and cold. When he saw what it was he nearly fell off. The ledge already had an occupant: a grinning, shrunken corpse.

Its leathery skin stretched taut over a weirdly narrow skull. Pebbles in its eye sockets were white in the moonlight. Its shrivelled lips were drawn back to reveal sharp yellow fangs.

'What is it?' called Renn.

Torak didn't answer. He'd spotted another ledge on the other side of the cleft – and above it several more, hacked in the rock. They went all the way to the top, and on each ledge crouched a wizened corpse, its skeletal arms clutching bony knees. The whole cave was thronged with the dead.

Then he noticed something else. One corpse was missing its head, another its foot. His own silent companion lacked its right hand, neatly chopped off at the wrist. He didn't know what this meant, but it was all too plain that the Kelp Clan had gone to enormous lengths to preserve their ancestors. They would not forgive those who desecrated their dead.

'What is it?' Renn cried again.

Tersely, he told her. She was silent for a moment. 'Are they fresh?' she called.

'I don't think so!' he said with a jittery laugh. A fresh corpse is dangerous because if the souls are still near, they might try to possess the living. How like Renn to think of that now.

He glanced from her to the ledge. Space enough for them both, as well as the corpse: they could make things right with the Kelp Clan later. For now, the dead must get along with the living.

'It's an easy climb!' he assured her. 'You can do it!'

The tide was rising fast, the Sea already churning round her ankles. Soon it would sweep her off the rocks. 'Renn? You have to do this!'

Reaching for a finger-hold with her good hand, she put her foot in a crack and heaved herself higher.

Torak leant down as far as he could. 'Grab my hand, you're nearly there!'

'I – can't reach!' she gasped.

'Yes, you can!'

But she couldn't. And they were both at full stretch.

A massive surge crashed into the cave, drenching them in spray. Renn's eyes were huge in her upturned face. 'You go on,' she panted.

'I'm not leaving you!'

'You've got to! Climb out, fetch help!'

'It'll be too late, the Sea will have taken you!'

Somehow he made his way back to her. For the last part he found himself groping for footholds in freezing water above his knees. 'You'll be safe on that ledge,' he told her firmly. 'You go first, I'll be right below you, I won't let you fall!'

Doggedly she did as he said. He hated to see her so obedient, her bright spirit quenched.

She was almost there. Bracing his legs, he grabbed her hips and boosted her onto the ledge. At the same moment the Sea roared in and tried to carry him away.

Renn scrambled aside to make room for him, nearly knocking the corpse off the ledge. 'Hurry!' she cried.

But now it was Torak who was shivering uncontrollably. The Sea was swirling round his thighs, his legs were going numb, his sodden clothes dragging him down.

Renn was shouting his name but the Sea was drowning her voice.

He stared up at her. No feeling in his fingers. He couldn't cling on for much longer.

He saw her lips mouth, *No!* It flashed across his mind that he was going to die. He would never see her again.

'Stay on the ledge!' he yelled. 'You'll be safe there! Wait till the tide turns – then climb down and get out of here! Renn, I—' The Sea Mother snatched the breath from his chest.

'*Torak!*' screamed Renn.

'I'm – sorry,' he tried to say. 'I love you...'

His thoughts were getting foggy. And now warmth was stealing through him and the cave was filling with gurgling laughter. It no longer sounded menacing, but strangely enticing – and he was so *sleepy*, he longed to go to the Sea Mother...

...to drift for ever in her vast embrace.

FOURTEEN

Renn heard a distant clamour of seagulls. Much nearer, women were murmuring and a baby was crying.

Hazily, she became aware that she was lying naked beneath a warm covering made of the softest feathers. Her hand and forearm were wrapped in what smelt like wet seaweed. The pain was gone. So was the fever.

Through half-open eyes she realized that she was in a small, dim tent. It seemed to be made of the shiny black bone which some whales have instead of teeth.

A girl in a seal-hide robe sat beside her. She had the reddened, weirdly narrow face of the Kelp Clan, and two white blobs instead of eyebrows, which gave her a startled look. Her hair was gathered in a topknot, and though she appeared to be about Renn's age, her frizzled grey locks were those of an old woman. Gripping a kelp-stem tube between her lips, she was passing the other end over Renn's body, making swift sucking sounds, then turning aside to blow into a rawhide pouch; perhaps to draw off the last traces of fever.

'Her colour's better,' wheezed an old woman whom Renn couldn't see.

'Pity she's so ugly,' murmured the girl with the grey topknot.

'All Easterners look like that,' said a woman's voice which sounded vaguely familiar.

'But her *head*!' said a child's voice. 'Ugh, it's *round*!'

'Her mate's not bad-looking,' said the old woman. 'Shame his mother didn't file his teeth.'

Torak. Renn's eyes flew open. 'Where's Torak!' she cried, struggling to sit up.

'He's fine,' the girl with the topknot assured her. 'He's in the other healing hut. Rest! You're still weak.'

When Renn next woke, the dressing had been taken off her arm, and three women and a child were leaning over her. All had the sharpened fangs and narrow red features of the Kelp Clan, and she recognized one as Halut, who'd been stranded with the Ravens after the Thunderstar. The child beside her was clearly her daughter; her shaven scalp was caked in earthblood, and with her white brow-blobs she resembled a small, solemn toadstool.

'What happened?' mumbled Renn. 'How did you find us?'

'The Ancestors summoned us to their cave with smoke,' the girl with the topknot said gravely.

Renn remembered the leathery corpse she'd nearly knocked off the ledge. 'I'm sorry. We didn't know they were there.'

The women took that in unnerving silence.

Renn realized that the baby was still grizzling. The girl with the topknot reached behind her and jiggled a birch-bark basket; the grizzling diminished to hiccuping sobs.

'My name is Elupalee,' said the girl. 'Halut you know. This is her daughter, Yamna. This is Lathren.' She indicated the old woman.

'We're not sure we did right by saving you,' said Halut, fingering a long bone amulet at her throat. 'Maybe the Ancestors want us to punish you instead.'

'Why did you come to our island?' wheezed Lathren, clutching a bowl of earthblood in her lap.

'We're looking for our pack-brother,' said Renn. 'He's a wolf, he was swept out to Sea on an iceberg. Have you seen him? Maybe heard howls?'

Yamna looked shifty, and Halut and the old woman cast uncertain glances at Elupalee, who smoothed her robe over her lap and gave Renn a sharp-fanged smile. 'Is it true that you and your mate live with wolves?'

Renn was puzzled. 'Halut knows we do.'

'I only know that you *say* you do,' Halut said coolly. 'I never actually saw you with a wolf.'

113

'You see,' said Elupalee, scratching her topknot, 'we don't know if you're telling the truth.'

'Why would I lie?' said Renn.

Elupalee turned to Lathren. 'My Ancestor's not giving me an answer. What about yours?'

The old woman shook her head. 'I think he wants us to get her dressed.'

With gentle insistence they helped Renn into a jerkin and under-leggings of squirrel fur, and socks made from the felted underfur of dogs. Over that went a parka and leggings of eider duck skin with the black-and-white feathers left on. Renn's clan-creature feathers had been sewn on the parka, which was brightly decorated with braided fish skin dyed red, yellow and blue. She didn't like that at all. How could she hunt if the prey could see her coming from a daywalk away?

To her relief they gave her back her gauntlets, her long seal-hide boots and the rest of her gear, including her Mage's belt, her medicine pouch, and Fin-Kedinn's wrist-guard. But not her weapons – except for her slingshot, which they didn't seem to realize *was* a weapon. When she asked for her axe and knife, she was met with blank stares.

'You won't be needing them any more,' said Halut.

'Why not?' Renn said uneasily.

Lathren patted her hand. 'Now to make you more wolf-like!' The old woman insisted on tying back Renn's hair so that her face appeared narrower, and cutting her fingernails to points; but when she offered to smear Renn's skin with earthblood, Renn politely declined. Her refusal became firmer when Lathren tried to file her teeth.

'At least let me pluck out your eyebrows,' the old woman pleaded, waving a pair of clam-shell tweezers.

'No,' said Renn, increasingly rattled.

Lathren flung up her hands. 'She refuses to be helped!'

'You've already improved her looks quite a lot,' Elupalee said reassuringly. 'And her mate is really quite wolf-like.' She turned to Renn. 'Have you made a baby with him?'

'No!' snapped Renn.

'Why not?'

'What's that to you?' Neither she nor Torak wanted a child: they didn't want to risk it as they both had Soul-Eater marrow; but she had no intention of telling these women.

Lathren was tut-tutting. 'She'll come to her senses! And when she does, I'll teach her to bind its head, so it'll grow up beautiful.'

'Like this!' Proudly, Elupalee tilted the basket to display her baby, which had finally fallen asleep. Its wrinkled red features were squashed between two wooden boards strapped tightly across the brow. The boards were well padded with moss, but they clearly hurt.

Renn was aghast. 'How can you do that to your own baby?'

The women's smiles stiffened.

'This is the way of our Ancestors,' said Lathren, affronted.

'It's no worse than the clan-tattoos you Easterners put on your children,' said Halut.

'We do that when they're seven,' retorted Renn. 'We don't hurt babies!'

The women exchanged shocked glances.

'The Ancestors don't like that at all,' declared Lathren.

'How do you know?' said Renn.

'Because they're here, of course!' cried Elupalee. She lifted her topknot clean off her head, revealing a shaven scalp caked in earthblood. 'This hair belonged to my grandmother!'

'This was my brother.' Halut touched her bone amulet.

'My father!' Lathren raised her bowl, which was the upper half of a man's skull, painted with wavy blue lines.

Renn stared at Halut in horror. 'You never told us you did this!'

Halut tightened her lips. 'You wouldn't have understood.'

Renn had had enough. 'I want to see Torak right now!'

'That's probably best,' Elupalee said curtly. 'Maybe he can talk some sense into you!'

Renn emerged blinking into the daylight and an eye-watering reek of fish.

In front of a second healing hut, a group of Kelp men stopped talking and stared at her. Their seal-hide clothes were edged in yellow and green, their wovenbark caps stained blue. All had the powerful shoulders and bandy legs of men who paddle more than they walk, and their fangs flashed white in their beardless red faces.

Lathren gave Renn a push. 'Go to your mate!'

Now the men were standing aside and Torak was running towards her and sweeping her into his arms. 'They wouldn't let me see you!' he said into her hair. 'How d'you feel?'

'I'm fine,' she mumbled against his chest.

Gripping her shoulders, he put her from him and studied her. Some of the tension left his face. 'You look better.'

She nodded. 'Fever's gone. And they've healed my hand.'

They locked gazes, and suddenly they were back in the cave in that terrible moment when the Sea was about to separate them for ever.

'I thought I'd never see you again,' he said. His eyes went to the freckle at the corner of her mouth, and she knew that he wanted to kiss her. She wanted it too – but not with half the Kelp Clan looking on.

Drawing her aside, he said under his breath, 'These people are *weird*! They never go into their Forest further than they can cast a harpoon! They think it belongs to ghosts!'

'And they squash their babies' heads,' whispered Renn. *'And they wear bits of their dead!'*

'They've taken my weapons. And have you noticed, the clothes they've given us are different from theirs?' For the first time Renn realized that he was splendidly but impractically dressed in white whale hide, stained purple at sleeves and hem. 'Whale hide's fragile,' he said. 'Tears like a leaf. What d'you think it means?'

'I don't know, but birdskin doesn't last long either.' She told him what the women had said about their ancestors. 'I think they're trying to decide whether to save us or punish us.'

'And they know something about Wolf, I'm sure of it!'

'I think so too.'

They glanced back at the two groups of Kelps, the women and the men, who stood by the healing huts, watching impassively.

The Kelp Clan settlement occupied a wide bay backed by dense Forest. At this end of the bay a river flowed into the Sea, and several magnificent canoes rocked in the shallows. In form they resembled those of the Sea-eagles, but were painted in searing designs of yellow, blue and red. Near them lay piles of fishing spears, herring rakes and nets.

Along the riverbank women were gutting baskets of herring. Dogs prowled for scraps, gulls swooped over reeking shell middens. Beyond these, in smoke-huts made of whale ribs, herrings and strings of clams dangled on racks, and boys tended fires. Further down the shore, girls laboured at cooking-pits ringed with white clam shells: Renn guessed that the shells had been set there so that people could avoid the pits in the dark.

Suddenly she realized what was missing. 'Where are their shelters?'

'Over there.' Torak pointed at a line of low, turf-covered mounds near the Forest. 'They live underground. Climb in through the roof.' His voice dropped to a whisper. 'They've shown me all over their camp, but they won't let me anywhere near that.' With his eyes he indicated a high log wall at the far end of the bay. 'They're definitely hiding something!'

Renn made to reply, but just then a hatch opened in the nearest mound and a young Kelp man poked out his narrow red head. 'Come inside,' he called to them with grave ceremony. 'Our Leader, Chinoot, desires your presence at the feast.'

FIFTEEN

Renn followed Torak down a log ladder into a dim, earth-smelling chamber thronged with people sitting cross-legged in expectant silence.

Inside it was surprisingly roomy, although the low whale-rib roof was festooned with outer clothing hung to dry: Renn could stand upright, but Torak had to stoop. She noticed a muscle tensing in his jaw. He hated confined places.

The walls of the shelter were faced with split logs painted in wavy green lines to resemble kelp, the floor was crunchy with dried seaweed. On a sleeping platform at one end, children nestled under elk pelts. None of them wore head-boards: presumably the babies were in another shelter, so they wouldn't disturb the feast.

The only light came from a great stone dish carved in the shape of a whale. It contained a thin layer of mashed blubber which sent up a flickering line of flame, and ankle-deep in the blubber stood the blue slate image of an extraordinary creature. It had stubby legs, a muzzle like a fox, and ears as big as a hare's. Renn guessed it was the Kelps' idea of a wolf, carved by someone who'd never seen one.

The blubber lamp cast a smoky glimmer on a man sitting beside it. His Mage's belt was braided kelp dyed yellow and fringed with puffin beaks, and on his breast hung a whale tooth as big as his fist. His jerkin and leggings were seal hide dyed green and trimmed with tassels of grey human hair. Renn wondered whose it had been, and when they'd died.

The man's clipped silver beard contrasted vividly with his reddened skin. He wore a headband of short upstanding feathers dyed yellow, and his scalp was shaved, except for one extremely long silver lock, hanging from the crown of his head, down his back, and tied around his waist.

Motioning Torak and Renn to sit, he appraised them with penetrating dark eyes as he fingered one of the tassels on his jerkin; Renn guessed that he was communing with his ancestor. 'I am Chinoot,' he said proudly. 'Leader and Mage of the Kelp Clan.'

Renn bowed. 'I'm Renn of the Raven Clan.'

'And I'm Torak. I don't have a clan, but I'm kin to the Seals, my mother—'

'I can tell you have salt in your marrow,' Chinoot cut in. 'Why did you come to our island?'

'We're looking for our pack-brother,' said Torak. 'A great grey wolf. Have you seen him?'

People murmured and stirred. Chinoot silenced them with an upraised hand. 'Our island is blessed by the Ancestors,' he said with an edge to his voice, 'but to our shame, no wolves live here now.'

'We know that,' said Renn. 'But—'

'Wolves did live here once,' the Leader went on as if she hadn't spoken. 'They taught the First Ancestors how to talk, how to live in clans and mate for life. Then one day a thoughtless boy threw a stone at a she-wolf, and they were offended. They went under the waves and became Sea wolves. That has been our worst misfortune.'

'So is Wolf here on your island?' Torak said impatiently.

'They say you know the speech of wolves,' said Chinoot. 'Can that be true?'

'Surely Halut's told you,' said Torak. 'What are you hiding?'

The Leader gave him a chilly smile, and Renn saw with alarm that his fangs were inlaid with glinting shards of mussel shell. 'Nothing is hidden from those who are pure of heart. Time for us to eat.'

'No, I need to know now!' cried Torak.

Renn gripped his arm. 'Why can't you just tell us?' she asked Chinoot.

'Time to eat,' he repeated. With a painted staff he

rapped on a roof-beam, and the hatch opened and women lowered baskets of steaming food.

While Torak sat seething, Chinoot filled a small greenstone bowl as an offering to the Sea Mother, and another for the Ancestors. Then he gave a bowl each to Torak and Renn, with a mussel-shell spoon. His expression was resolute. They had no choice but to obey.

Besides, the food was delicious. There were clams steamed in their own juices, stone-fried turbot and tender crabmeat slathered in hot seal oil; sweet black cakes of crisp dried rockweed; and a wonderfully refreshing orange mash of sea buckthorn berries. Renn couldn't get enough of one dish she'd never had before: broad greenish-brown strips of some kind of crunchy dried seaweed, coated in a wonderful fishy grey crust.

She asked what it was, and Chinoot said it was dried herring eggs on kelp. 'Ah, but you should taste it when it's fresh!' he smiled, unbending a little. 'In two moons the herring will spawn, and coat the Forest under the Sea with their roe three fingers thick! We have only to go out in our canoes and rake it in. It's such a blessing!'

Torak nudged Renn with his elbow. 'D'you realize what this means?' he hissed. 'This is *kelp*! They're *eating* their clan-creature!'

She stopped munching. 'That'd be like me eating Rip or Rek!' she whispered.

Chinoot had overheard. 'Our ways are not your ways,' he said with a shrug. 'Halut tells me that you Easterners eat mushrooms; that's something we never do. Mushrooms are the food of ghosts.'

The feast wore on and at last Chinoot gave a sign and the dishes were taken away. Placing his hands on his knees, he fixed Torak and Renn in turn with his keen dark gaze. 'A few days ago,' he began, 'another Easterner came to our island. He too was seeking a wolf. He too said it was his pack-brother, and that he could talk its speech—'

'Naiginn,' snarled Renn.

'You know him?' said the Leader.

'Where is he?' cried Torak. 'What did you tell him?'

'*He* was courteous,' Chinoot said drily. 'He too said that he was kin to the Seal Clan – and we knew this was true, as he was the finest skinboater we've ever seen. We welcomed him, as we welcome all strangers—'

'Oh, Naiginn's very persuasive,' Renn said bitterly. 'He's also an ice demon in human form.'

'Where is he?' demanded Torak.

'We soon sensed that he was lying,' said Chinoot, 'so we sent him on his way. But you're mistaken, he is no demon.'

'Yes, he is,' retorted Renn.

Chinoot drew himself up. 'There are no demons on our island! From the Beginning, when the Sea Mother sang the world into existence, our Ancestors have protected us! Just as they protected us from the Thunderstar that ravaged *your* land in the East.'

'Naiginn *is* a demon,' insisted Renn. 'And he wants to kill Wolf!'

Yamna squealed in distress. The rest of the clan murmured in outrage. Chinoot clasped the tassel of human hair and frowned. 'As I told you, we sent the Easterner on his way. I had intended to do the same to you – until I saw that.' He pointed at Torak's little slate wolf on its thong at his throat. 'Where did you get it?'

'My friend Dark made it for me. But what—'

'Ah, the White Raven. Halut has spoken of him. She said he healed her brothers' burns after the Thunderstar.'

'You can't possibly think that Naiginn's really gone?' Renn broke in.

Chinoot bristled. 'I told him to leave. He had no choice.'

'He's a *demon!*' exclaimed Torak. 'He's after Wolf, he'll stay on this island till he's found him!'

The Leader made to reply, but suddenly Yamna flung down her bowl. 'Why can't we *tell* them?' she burst out. 'He won't eat, he won't sleep, all he does is pace! He's so *unhappy!*'

'Who?' Torak leapt to his feet, nearly braining himself on a roof-beam.

'Perhaps the child is right,' mused Chinoot. 'Perhaps this is why the Ancestors saved them—'

'*Who is she talking about?*' shouted Torak.

The Leader raised his eye-blobs at his discourtesy. 'Why, the wolf,' he said.

The Kelps had built a platform on their side of the wall of logs, so that they could see into the pen. 'You must stay here with us,' Chinoot warned Torak and Renn. 'Only Yamna may go down into the pen, the wolf won't tolerate anyone else—'

But Torak and Renn had already scrambled over the wall, and Wolf was hurtling towards them. Torak was on his knees, burying his face in his pack-brother's scruff and Wolf was nuzzling his neck, whimpering ecstatically, flailing his forepaws and waggling his hindquarters: *Pack-brother! I knew you'd come!*

Tearing himself away, Wolf raced to Renn and knocked her over with snuffle-licks, then dashed back to Torak. It was only then that Torak saw the state he was in. Wolf's flanks were scrawny, with bare patches where he'd torn out clumps of fur. Worst of all, his tail was clamped between his legs – he hadn't wagged it once – and when Torak touched his rump he yelped.

Torak noticed the trampled mud at the foot of the wall where Wolf had paced to and fro. In places he'd chewed the bark off the logs, and claw-marks higher up told of his doomed attempts to escape.

'*What have you done to him?*' Torak roared at the Kelps, who'd been watching in awe from the platform.

'We *saved* him!' Chinoot retorted angrily.

'Imprisoning him? Starving him?' Torak flung back. 'Can't you see he's desperate? He belongs in a Forest, not a pen!'

126

'We saved his *life*!' Yamna cried in a choked voice. 'I heard ravens calling, I found him drowning in quicksand!'

'What did you do to his tail?' cried Torak.

'He must have strained it swimming ashore,' said Chinoot. 'This happens to our dogs if they swim too much.'

Renn was carefully probing Wolf's hindquarters. 'I think he's right,' she told Torak. 'It isn't broken, only strained.'

'He'll be better in a few days,' said Chinoot. 'And he'll start to eat again now that you're here.'

For the first time Torak noticed three wovenroot baskets lying in the mud. One was piled with crabs, another with octopus, the third held half a cod. The food was untouched, except for a few peck-marks; but a granite trough of clean water was ringed with paw-prints. The Kelps had even built a Wolf-sized shelter of spruce boughs, lined with moss for a comfortable bed.

Torak felt slightly ashamed of his outburst. 'I can see you've done your best,' he said grudgingly, 'and we are grateful. But now we have to get back to the Forest.'

'He means *our* Forest in the east,' put in Renn. 'It's where Wolf belongs.'

Chinoot stood in thoughtful silence; but Yamna's small face twisted with grief. '*No!*'

'Hush,' said her mother. 'The Leader won't let it happen!'

Torak spoke to Chinoot. 'We'll be needing a boat. Ours was holed by black ice—'

'We know,' Chinoot said haughtily. 'We found it.'

'Then we don't need to trouble you any more,' said Renn. 'Once we've repaired our canoe, we'll be on our way.'

The Leader bared his teeth in a glinting smile. 'Oh, you won't be needing a canoe. From now on you'll be living with us.'

Torak and Renn stared at him.

'At last it's clear to me why the Ancestors saved you,' the Kelp Leader went on. 'They want you to stay on our island and help us care for our wolf.'

'He's not your wolf,' growled Torak.

'Yes, he is,' replied Chinoot. 'The Sea Mother gave him to us.'

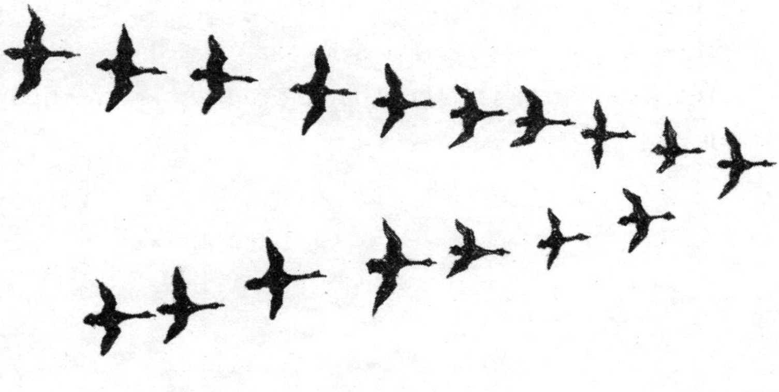

SIXTEEN

'But our island is so much *better* than your Forest in the East!' insisted Chinoot. 'The Sea Mother sends us fish, seals, whales, kelp! The shore gives us octopus and clams, the trees provide canoes. Our brave dogs venture inland and chase out the deer for us to hunt! Why would you *want* to live anywhere else?'

'It's not our home,' Renn said wearily.

Torak sat beside her in glowering silence; she could sense that he was on the brink of losing his temper.

They'd been arguing all day, and as night fell Chinoot had ordered everyone back to the shelter. Wolf had gone wild when they'd left, yowling and hurling himself at the wall. Torak had told him they'd be back soon, but in wolf talk there is no future, and he wasn't sure that Wolf had understood.

'Wolf has a *mate*,' Renn told Chinoot. 'Any day now she's going to have cubs!'

The Leader raised his painted eye-blobs. 'How do I know you're not making that up?'

'But you can see how miserable he is!' cried Torak. 'Yamna told me he hasn't howled once!'

'He'll be better now that you're here – and when he does howl, it will be a *great* blessing on us all.'

Renn tried another approach. 'This island is the home of your Ancestors,' she began. 'And the Forest in the East is the home of *ours*. My fa's bones lie in my clan's bone-grounds on the Windriver. The bones of Torak's parents lie elsewhere. It's the same for Wolf. It's not *right* that you're keeping us from our Ancestors!'

A few people looked troubled, but Chinoot remained unmoved. 'The Sea Mother gave the wolf to *us*! Now she has sent you to help care for him. That's *why* she holed your canoe, that's *why* the Ancestors rescued you!'

'But they *didn't*!' exploded Torak. 'That smoke you saw came from a fire *I woke*!'

'Because the Ancestors let you,' Chinoot replied with infuriating calm.

The hatch creaked open and two brawny young Kelps climbed down the log ladder. Chinoot went to speak to them in private.

While he was gone, Torak whispered in Renn's ear: 'I've had enough of this!'

'Yes, but what do we do?' she breathed. 'How do we get Wolf away from an entire clan? Even if we manage that – *and* steal a canoe – they'd catch us in no time! And if we escape into the Forest, we'd have to make a skinboat to get off the island; we'd have the same problem.'

'I still think it's worth a try. They never go into their Forest, and even if they did they'd be no match for us. It's better than doing nothing, waiting for Naiginn to attack Wolf!'

She nodded. 'If we guessed the Kelps were hiding Wolf, so will he. He'll be lying low somewhere, trying to work out where he is.'

Torak stirred restlessly. 'Well, if Chinoot thinks I'm going to sleep in here while Wolf is alone in that pen…'

'Agreed. As soon as they're all asleep we'll—'

'Sh! He's coming back!'

The Leader brought the young men with him. His face was grim. 'You were right,' he said. 'The stranger called Naiginn: he said he was going to Cormorant Island – but he lied.'

'We found traces of his camp on the north coast,' said one of the young men. 'He was gone, but…' His face puckered in distress. 'He'd killed a porpoise. He'd eaten the head and left the rest to rot!'

'Now do you understand?' Renn said to Chinoot. 'Only a demon would violate the Pact!'

'He's after Wolf,' insisted Torak. 'He thinks if he eats Wolf's head while he's still alive, it will set him free.'

The Kelps cried out in horror and clutched their Ancestor amulets, but Chinoot remained inscrutable, fingering his tassel of grey human hair. 'This is indeed a terrible evil,' he said at last. 'But it changes *nothing*. It merely shows the wisdom of the Sea Mother and our Ancestors in bringing you here, where no demon can hurt you.'

'What it shows,' Torak said between his teeth, 'is that Wolf can't stay here any longer! At any moment Naiginn could catch him in that pen like a weasel in a trap!'

'Oh, there's no danger of that,' said Chinoot with a wave of his hand. 'Our dogs would never allow an attack from the Forest – and if the demon tried to come from the Sea, his boat would be wrecked on the boulders which our Ancestors hid in the shallows: only we know the secret way in.'

'You don't know Naiginn,' said Torak.

'You have no idea how cunning he is,' said Renn.

'Enough!' Chinoot struck the ground twice with his staff. 'I have decided. The wolf stays with us – and so do you!'

The last Kelp had fallen asleep, and Torak followed Renn up the log ladder.

It creaked as she lifted the hatch. She froze. Someone turned over in their sleep – and went on snoring. Renn rolled her eyes. Torak exhaled.

To their relief the camp was in darkness, no one about except for a boy by the smoke-huts nodding drowsily by the fire. A dog wandered over and sniffed Torak, then padded off into the gloom. Some of the tension left his body. That dog wouldn't be so calm if a demon was near.

The tide was out, waves quietly lapping the shore. A cold clear night, the moon a few days off full. This made it easy to follow the clam shells bordering the path that led to Wolf's pen. As Renn vaulted onto the platform, a raven flew onto the wall and gurgled a greeting. 'So there you are!' she whispered to Rip.

Torak boosted her over the wall, then chucked her their sleeping-sacks and dropped into the pen. Softly he whined to Wolf: *Pack-brother! It's us!*

No Wolf came racing from the shadows. No Wolf...

'He's gone,' said Torak in disbelief.

'Are you sure?' breathed Renn.

He was about to reply when a small figure moved in the darkness. It was Yamna. Her eyes were gleaming with excitement.

'Where is he?' hissed Torak.

'I set him free!' The child pointed at Wolf's spruce-bough shelter, which she'd dragged against the wall of the pen so that Wolf could escape.

Torak rubbed a hand over his face.

'Did – I do wrong?' faltered Yamna.

He didn't reply. Wolf was out there in the Forest, oblivious of the threat, and with no pack-brother to protect him. And Naiginn could be anywhere.

SEVENTEEN

Wolf leapt onto a fallen pine and sniffed the rich scents of prey streaming over his nose.

What a relief to be back among trees! He'd left the fish-smelling taillesses far behind, and the Great Wet could growl as much as she liked, she couldn't catch him here. Soon Tall Tailless and the pack-sister would find him and they would go back to the Forest where Darkfur was waiting, and the pack would be together again.

As Wolf raced up the slope he smelt badger and hare, elk, marten, deer. He also caught a faint whiff of demon, but it was so far off he decided to ignore it.

The prey too was many lopes away, and although the

moss beneath the trees was scattered with fish bones, they'd all been picked clean. Wolf found an egg fallen from its nest and crunched it up, but it only made him hungrier. He thought with longing of the juicy fish and giant spiders he'd left at the Den of the taillesses. If only he'd stopped to eat before escaping over the wall.

The Dark turned to Light and as he paused to drink from a little Fast Wet, he wondered if he should turn back and find Tall Tailless and the pack-sister.

In the Up the ravens that belonged to the pack were excitedly cawing. An eagle was flying this way and that to avoid them, and they were trying to steal the fish wriggling in its talons. The eagle was heading for its nest high in a spruce, but the ravens were harrying it relentlessly, it was getting tired. Next time they attacked, it dropped the fish.

Not even the ravens were quick enough to catch the prize, which plummeted into the Forest – but Wolf had seen where it fell and was loping uphill. As he ran he heard the ravens flying overhead, he felt the eagle's wingbeats ruffling his fur…

Next moment he found the fish. The ravens circled, loudly complaining, the eagle swooped to snatch the fish. Snarling, Wolf stood over it: *Go away, it's mine!* Again the eagle swooped. Wolf snapped – tail-feathers drifted to earth – and with an angry shriek the great bird headed for its nest, where its mate screamed at it for losing her food.

Wolf gobbled the juicy fish, uttering muffled growls to ward off the ravens. Now he felt *much* better. After trampling a sleeping-spot in the moss, he curled up for a nap.

When he woke, the ravens had picked the fish bones clean and were perched on a stump, pecking lice from each other's necks.

Wolf took several luxuriant stretches and yawned. He shut his muzzle with a snap. On the wind he'd caught two much-loved scents.

Whimpering with joy, he raced downhill to find Tall Tailless and the pack-sister.

The flurry of greetings was over and Torak knelt in the moss beside his pack-brother, who'd taken his arm in a slobbery jaw-hold and was tasting his new clothes.

The pale-pelted demon, Torak told him in wolf talk. *Can you smell him?*

Wolf released Torak's arm and sneezed. *Not sure, scent's very faint.*

The demon is hunting you, Torak said urgently. *You must* not *attack!*

Wolf glanced at him, his amber eyes puzzled. Doubtfully he swung his tail. *But hunting demons is what Wolf is for.*

Not this time, said Torak. Much *danger!*

His pack-brother cocked his head. *There's always danger.*

This is different. If the demon comes near, you must *stay hidden!*

Sensing his agitation, Wolf put his forehead against

Torak's. Torak shut his eyes and sank his hands into his pack-brother's scruff, inhaling his beloved sweet-grass scent.

'Does he understand?' asked Renn.

'I don't think so,' said Torak.

'What does he say about Naiginn? Is he anywhere near?'

'He says the scent's very faint.'

'Let's hope it stays that way.'

Torak didn't reply. If he could keep Wolf safely out of the way, he *wanted* Naiginn to find them. He was determined to bring this to an end.

The Forest on this side of the island was slightly less impassable than in the west, and after leaving the Kelp Clan camp he and Renn had followed the river upstream. Wolf had burst upon them around daybreak, when they'd stopped to take stock of their gear and decide what to do.

As well as the deerhide sleeping-sacks they'd brought from camp, Torak had his seal-gut waterskin under his parka and Renn the little pouch of smoked herring; both had their tinder and medicine pouches – but no weapons, except for slingshots.

'And they're not much use in Forest this dense,' grumbled Renn.

'I wish I'd been able to steal an axe,' said Torak.

'And a *bow*!' Like him, she'd smeared herself all over with mud to make her light-coloured clothes less conspicuous. Now she was untying her hair and shaking it out.

It was warmer in this part of the Forest, a smell of spring

in the air. Birches and rowans were waking up, and finches chattered in the pines. A short way upstream, Torak found the remains of an elk. Elk bone is hard and splinters to very sharp points; he split a couple of ribs with a rock and they settled down to make knives.

Torak chose a vicious-looking shard and secured it to a sturdy stick with raw pine-blood, which would harden as it dried. He bound it on with half the spare bowstring Renn always wore round her calf; she said the Kelp women had left it untouched, thinking it was something to do with Magecraft.

Searching the undergrowth, Torak found an even better weapon, a broken piece of red deer antler half-buried in moss. The knobby end where it had grown from the skull was rock-hard, it would make a formidable club, and at the other end was a lethal spike. Good for gouging, he thought grimly.

Wolf returned from exploring upstream and touched noses with him, then with Renn. His tail was up, his muzzle relaxed. This told Torak that Naiginn couldn't be anywhere close.

It was already past noon. Warm enough in the sun by the stream, but icy in the shade. As Torak and Renn shared a slip of smoked herring, Rip and Rek appeared out of nowhere and stalked about, hoping for scraps.

'I don't think we need worry about the Kelps,' said Torak. 'They're afraid of the Forest, they won't dare come after us.'

'They won't need to,' Renn pointed out. 'They know we can't stay in here for ever. And Naiginn will be looking for Wolf.'

'That's what I'm hoping,' said Torak. 'I want him to find us, and I want it to be here in the Forest, not at Sea where he has the advantage.'

She made to protest, but he talked over her. 'We have to end this now, Renn! I'm sick of skulking about hoping he won't attack! We have to make him come to us!'

'How d'you intend to do that?'

'Do a summoning charm. Do it now!'

'No,' she said flatly.

'Why not?'

She thrust her new knife in her belt. 'For one thing, I don't have any earthblood.'

'You have those strands of his hair. Surely they'd be enough—'

'I said no.'

'Why?'

'Torak, you know why! Because I will not let you become outcast! And I've no idea how to banish his souls!'

'So *what*?' he cried in a voice that made Wolf set back his ears. 'If he's dead, he can't go after Wolf!'

'What if his souls got into something else? What if they got into a bear?'

He stared at her. 'Demons can't just slip into whatever creature they like!'

'You're sure about that, are you? Because I'm not, not with an ice demon as powerful as Naiginn!'

He crossed his arms on his chest. 'So what d'you think we should do?'

'Lie low and make a boat: deerhide if we have to, or steal one from the Kelps. Then try to get home. It's all we *can* do.'

No, it isn't, Torak told her silently. Out loud he said, 'Fine, we'll do it your way. We'll steal a boat.'

Her dark eyes narrowed suspiciously. 'It's not like you to give in so easily.'

He forced a laugh. 'Well, this time I have! Although I'm pretty sure the Kelps will guess we'll be after a canoe, so I think we should hide out here for a couple of days before we try. Yes?'

Slowly she nodded.

He could see that she'd guessed he wasn't telling her everything – and she was right. But if she'd known what he was planning, she'd have tried to stop him.

A couple of days in the Forest should give him all the time he needed to do his own version of a summoning charm – without her noticing. And if his plan worked and he was able to lure Naiginn, then he could end this once and for all.

EIGHTEEN

'Dark soon,' said Torak. 'We need to find somewhere to camp.'

'Not here.' Renn wrinkled her nose at the rotten-egg stink rising from the hot spring. 'This water tastes awful!'

'And there are leeches.'

'Ugh, where?'

'Under these ferns. I think they've woken early because of the warmth. They're a lot bigger than the ones back home.'

Pulling back his sleeve, he found one almost a hand long, its suckers clamped to his forearm, its slug-like body swollen with blood. He flicked it off between finger and thumb, and Wolf despatched it with a snap before the ravens could get it.

'I'm definitely *not* camping here,' said Renn, checking inside her clothes.

'There's a deer trail up that hill.'

'Good, we'll find somewhere up there.'

The moment her back was turned, Torak whipped the stick from his belt and printed another paw-print in the mud. Anyone born in the Forest would know it for a fake; but Naiginn wasn't from the Forest, and with luck he'd be fooled.

All afternoon Torak had been leaving a false trail for the ice demon. Paw-prints in moss and mud, a tuft of Wolf's underfur snagged on a branch: the more obvious the better. Renn had no idea what he was doing – if she'd known about his 'summoning charm', she'd have tried to stop him – but he felt no guilt at deceiving her.

Halfway up the hill they found signs that a bear had woken from its winter sleep: skid-marks where it had slipped on a steep part, a pile of dung – fortunately, not fresh. Wolf had a roll in the dung, then he and Renn went on ahead. Torak seized his chance and left another tuft of fur on a bush.

He'd only just finished when Wolf came bounding down the trail, Renn following behind. 'We can't go any further,' she panted. 'Bear den's just behind those rocks!'

Annoyingly, they couldn't find a campsite at the bottom of the hill either. 'Unless you fancy a mud pool,' she grumbled. 'Or a pile of rotten stumps.'

A thrush was calling loudly in the deepening dusk, but

around them the spruce trees stood silent and still. Under one of them the ground was piled with cones nibbled clean by squirrels. High in the same tree, Torak made out the dark bulk of an eagles' nest: a bulky platform of branches as big as a canoe.

He pointed. 'Up there.'

Renn stared at him. 'What, camp in a nest?'

He shrugged. 'Plenty of room.'

'And you don't think the eagles will mind?'

'Can you see any fresh droppings? That nest hasn't been used in ages! And Naiginn can't climb trees.'

'He wouldn't need to, he could just set fire to it.'

'He won't know we're up there. Besides, a while ago you said you couldn't sense any demons.'

She chewed her lip. 'It'll be crawling with bird lice.'

'I told you, it's *abandoned*! No leeches either,' he added slyly.

That persuaded her.

The tree didn't mind being climbed, and the nest was even better than it appeared from the ground: solid as a rock, so dense that no one could spot them from below – and not a louse in sight. Also, the squirrels' midden around its roots was crunchy underfoot, a perfect warning if Naiginn approached.

Torak took the first watch, having privately decided not to wake Renn at all. Wrapping his sleeping-sack around him, he settled down to wait, hoping against hope that his false trail would lead the ice demon into his ambush.

The night was windless and almost mild, a few clouds drifting across the moon. Torak heard a flock of crossbills settle in the branches below the nest and feast on spruce cones, showering the ground with scales.

Wolf had gone off to hunt, and in a nearby tree Rip and Rek slept with their beaks tucked under their back feathers. Every so often Torak saw the glint of their eyes as they woke briefly and checked for danger. He lobbed a piece of herring as far as he could, and the ravens woke properly and flew after it. With luck they'd be gone a while. This was one night when he didn't want them raising the alarm if Naiginn approached.

Torak pictured himself dropping like a spider onto the ice demon: snapping his neck on impact, killing him instantly.

The next moment he thought, No, I don't want that, I want him to know it's me. I want to see the look in his eyes as I finish him off with my club...

It was disturbingly easy to imagine killing him – even if it meant killing him without warning, which would be breaking clan law. Torak found that he simply didn't care. Was it because he didn't have his medicine horn? Or had he always had this ruthlessness inside him, a dark seed waiting to grow?

He remembered Fin-Kedinn telling the tale of how evil had come into the world. In the first winter the World Spirit had battled the Great Auroch, fiercest of demons. The Spirit had won, but the wind had scattered the Evil

148

One's ashes, and a tiny speck had settled in the marrow of every creature.

'Evil exists in us all,' Fin-Kedinn had told Torak once. 'Some fight it, some feed it. That's how it's always been.' What would the Raven Leader say now, if he could see his foster son calmly contemplating killing a man? Because despite Naiginn's demon souls, he was still a man...

The crossbills flew off with shrill calls. Beneath the tree, a footstep crunched.

Scarcely daring to move, Torak peered over the edge of the nest.

Moonlight glinted in Naiginn's fair hair as he stooped to examine the ground at his feet.

It was the first time Torak had seen him since the ice demon had held him captive in the Deep Forest. He'd been beaten, bound, utterly in Naiginn's power. He remembered the scarred face and lightless stare, cold beyond imagining. He saw again Naiginn's fingers stroking his black flint knife as he eyed Torak's cheek, deciding where to make the first cut...

In the moonlight the bone harpoon on the ice demon's back gleamed faintly alongside his quiverful of arrows. It would take only one touch of that harpoon, or one arrowprick to stun Wolf into helplessness. Then the ice demon would devour his souls – and the brightest spirit in the Forest would be gone for ever.

All this flashed through Torak's mind in a heartbeat. Next moment he heard Renn stirring in her sleep. He shot her an agonized glance. She snuggled deeper into her sleeping-sack and went quiet.

Again Torak peered over the edge. He stifled a cry. Wolf was stalking Naiginn between the trees.

Naiginn hadn't yet seen him, but Wolf was only ten paces away, well within arrowshot. He was creeping closer with lowered head, placing each paw with silent care.

If ever Torak's spirit had called to his pack-brother, it called to him now. *Get back!* he screamed silently.

Wolf halted: ears rammed forwards, one forepaw raised. Lifting his head, he locked gazes with Torak.

Don't attack! Torak told him frantically in his mind. *Run!*

The amber gaze blinked out. Wolf disappeared into the Forest like mist.

But Naiginn was gone too.

NINETEEN

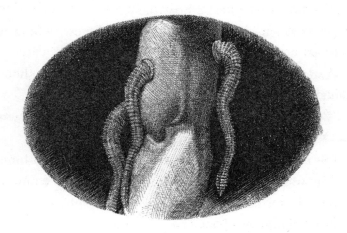

'Did something happen last night?' said Renn.

'No,' said Torak, looking as shifty as Wolf hiding a bone.

'Yes, it did,' she said.

'Then why ask?'

'Torak. Since daybreak you've been searching for tracks behind my back. What's going on?'

He hesitated. 'Last night I saw Naiginn.'

'*What?* Where?'

'Under our tree. But only for a moment.'

'Did you go after him?'

'Of course! But clouds covered the moon and I lost his trail. He was heading for the coast.'

'Which,' she said drily, 'is why we're heading there now.'

'Well, it makes sense: he hates the Forest, feels more in control by the Sea. And that's where he'll be hiding his boat.'

'The sooner *we* steal a boat the better,' said Renn. 'We need to get back to the Forest – *our* Forest, where we belong!'

'And then what? Wait for him to take another shot at Wolf?'

'We'll come up with something. At least we'll be with Fin-Kedinn – and Dark.'

His mouth hardened. 'You don't think I can beat him.'

She was about to reply when Wolf burst from the undergrowth, scattering them with dew. His eyes were bright, his muzzle bloody from a fresh kill.

'I reckon we're about half a daywalk from the Kelps,' said Renn, watching Torak stoop to acknowledge his pack-brother's greeting. 'I say we make for their camp and steal a canoe.'

'Right,' he said curtly.

The sun came out and the ground turned squelchy underfoot, but for once the Forest seemed to be helping, and they found a way south, a deer trail winding along a thickly wooded ravine.

Torak walked ahead, gripping his club; Renn could see the tension in his shoulders. This, she thought, is Naiginn's true evil: he spreads discord between us like a stain.

With a pang she watched a flock of crossbills flying

overhead. In two days it would be Egg Dawn, when winter turned to spring, and Mages collected crossbill eggs for their rites. And she didn't even have any earthblood for marking the Dawn.

It was greener at the bottom of the ravine, and they came to a strange place where the earth was honeycombed with enormous ferny hollows, as if giants had been throwing rocks. The hollows were very old: on the narrow ridges between them grew ancient yews, their scaly red roots snaking over boulders.

A woodpigeon flew off with a clatter of wings. After that, silence. Renn put her hand to her clan-creature feathers: she sensed that this place had power.

Rip alighted on a root near her. The raven's head-feathers were bristling, and for a moment his deep black gaze met hers: he felt it too.

Torak went ahead, picking his way along the ridges. As they were too narrow to walk abreast, Wolf went next, then Renn. She became aware of a faint high humming on the edge of hearing. The hairs on her forearms prickled. What she was sensing was the Nanuak: the raw power that pulses through all living things. For some reason it was very strong here.

Wolf, padding before her, turned his head to follow the movement of something she couldn't see. She pictured narrow-headed ghosts with fangs.

'That's odd,' Torak said softly, pointing into the nearest hollow. In the middle was a massive tree stump.

Its splayed roots were so smothered in moss that it resembled a huge green spider. 'That tree wasn't toppled by a storm,' he said. 'The stump's too flat. It was felled by people.'

'And there's the trunk.' Renn pointed into the adjacent hollow. 'Looks like they were making a dugout.' The trunk was also cloaked in moss, but they could still make out the broad furrow which had been hacked along its length by long-dead hands. 'I wonder why they never finished it,' she murmured.

Torak had scrambled down into the hollow on the other side and was exploring it with Wolf. 'Renn, this was a *camp*! Here's the remains of a shelter... And look, this was a grindstone!'

'But I thought the Ancestors lived on the coast.'

'Maybe not,' he mused. 'The Kelps said there used to be wolves on the island, but then they left. Maybe that's when the Ancestors moved to the coast, and started building their shelters underground. Maybe they couldn't bear living in a Forest without wolves. I know I couldn't.' He glanced up at her, the leaflight turning his eyes a silvery green. Then he shook himself. 'Well, that's in the past. Nothing we can do about it now.'

'No, wait. I think the Forest brought us here for a reason.'

'What d'you mean?'

Motioning him to silence, she broke off one of her clan-creature feathers and tucked it behind a root as an offering. Quietly, she addressed the spirits of the place.

'Thank you for letting us come here. Please show us what you want us to see, then let us leave in peace.'

A branch creaked. She felt a chill as the sun went in, a cloud passing across it like a hand.

In the hollow, Torak was sniffing the air. 'Smells like another hot spring. More leeches.' He raked his fingers over Wolf's flank and found one. 'Even so, I think I'll—'

Quite suddenly, his voice cut off and he wasn't there. Renn was still standing on the ridge but now it was summer, and everything had changed – and yet she wasn't afraid, for she knew that she was seeing this place as it had been long ago.

A peaceful camp full of busy, narrow-headed people: the Ancestors of the Kelps. Men and women alike were barefoot and bare-chested, wearing only calf-length leggings of supple wovenbark. Their skin was caked in earthblood, vivid red against the bright green ferns, and in their every gesture and glance Renn felt a powerful sense of togetherness and kinship: these were people who did everything together, and were content.

In the hollow to her left, two men were wielding slate adzes and hacking a groove along the length of an enormous log; she caught the tang of fresh tree-blood. Beyond them, beneath a boulder jutting from the side of the hollow, two more men were digging with antler picks. Close by, three girls were mashing salmon eggs on a grindstone. Children chased each other shrieking along the ridge, leaping lightly past Renn as if she wasn't there.

In the hollow to her right, a young woman sat cross-legged outside a deerhide shelter. Beside her was a pile of evenly-sized pebbles: she was making sink-stones for a fishing net. The pebble she held in her hand was egg-shaped, it had a hole in the middle for securing it to the net, and above this she was pecking two smaller dents with a rock, to make a face.

Raising her head, the woman calmly met Renn's gaze. Her eyes were the colour of the moon, and Renn's mind flashed back to the shrivelled Ancestor in the sea-cave whom she'd unceremoniously shoved aside. 'If that was you,' she told the woman with a bow, 'I'm sorry. I didn't mean to treat you with disrespect.'

The woman smiled, baring wolfish white fangs. 'It was me, but I accept your apology.' Holding the sink-stone to her eye, she peered at Renn. 'This will be needed, I think.'

'Is that why you let me see you?'

The woman put the stone in her lap and regarded Renn with grave sadness. 'Remember, the pain will end.'

'What do you mean?'

A man at the diggings called across to the woman and she turned her head to answer him – and faded into the ferns. The camp was gone. Renn found herself looking down at Torak.

'—go and fill the waterskin,' he said, flicking a leech off Wolf's flank.

The sun was going in, a cloud passing across it like a hand. Renn swallowed. She looked at the mossy tree-trunk in the hollow with its barely perceptible groove: the same trunk on which the men had been working with adzes.

'How many leeches have you taken off Wolf?' she asked Torak.

He blinked in surprise. 'Only one. Why?'

Only one leech… And that cloud had been in the same place the moment before her vision. It had lasted no longer than a heartbeat.

'What's the matter?' said Torak.

Renn had scrambled down into the hollow and was rooting around in the ferns. It didn't take her long to find what she was seeking: a pile of moss-covered pebbles, all roughly the same size. Perfect for sink-stones.

The topmost pebble was egg-shaped. With her knife she scraped it clean. It had a large hole in the middle, and above that two smaller dents had been hammer-pecked, for eyes. As Renn put it in her medicine pouch she wondered why the Ancestor had left it for her to find.

'Renn, what's this about?' demanded Torak.

'I had a vision of the Ancestors. I think I know why they camped here.'

Making her way to the other side of the hollow, she found the overhanging boulder where the men had been digging. Parting the ferns underneath, she found a wide gash in the red earth. It was just big enough to belly-crawl through, and opened out inside into a low cave. Bats hung from the roof like furry black fruit, and the walls were dark-red. Renn caught a familiar earthy tang.

'Earthblood!' she told Torak. 'Hand me your club so I can dig some out.'

'Not now, Renn, we need to get going!'

'Then don't, I'll use a rock.'

'Well, be quick, will you? I'm going to fill the waterskin, then I want to get moving!'

The hot spring was further off than Torak had thought, but he found it by its smell. Wolf came too, until its stink sent him sneezing back to Renn.

The spring bubbled up among boulders and made a fern-fringed pool before tumbling downhill. The pool was red with earthblood, the air above it quivering with heat.

Rip and Rek flew to the edge and had a vigorous bathe, their feathers flashing violet and green in a sparkle of droplets. Torak, squatting to fill his waterskin, found himself gazing into the name-souls of the overhanging pines. He munched a few fern tips and felt the peace of the place seeping into his spirit.

It took him a moment to notice the blood trickling down his wrist. 'Oh, not again,' he muttered. Reaching under his sleeve, he touched a fat worm-like body – and another. After pulling off his parka and jerkin, he found three bloated leeches clinging to his right arm and two more dangling from his breastbone. He dealt with these, then felt inside his leggings and picked another leech off his hip.

Rip and Rek shot into the air, uttering long rasping calls: raap – raap! *Intruder!*

Moments later Torak heard a rustling in the undergrowth as if some large creature, maybe an elk, was moving towards him.

But it wasn't an elk. It was Naiginn.

TWENTY

Naiginn didn't see Torak crouching behind the boulder, he was too busy clawing leeches from his neck. Snarling in disgust, he flung aside his weapons and yanked his parka and jerkin over his head, then tore off the bloated worms clinging to his chest.

Ever since Torak had first set eyes on Naiginn he'd been desperate to fight him, and he'd never had the chance. At last here he was, not three paces away on the other side of the pool. Swinging his club, Torak went for him. But Naiginn was quicker than a viper, snatching his axe and swinging back. Torak dodged. The axe-handle caught him a glancing blow on the forearm and he dropped the club. He lashed out with his knife. Naiginn parried the blow, twisted the knife from his grip and flung it into the ferns; then he found Torak's club and lobbed it down the slope. Squaring his shoulders, he grinned. He was broader than Torak and armed with harpoon, axe and knife; now Torak had nothing. Torak retreated to the other side of the pool to give himself time to think.

Rip and Rek had been diving at Naiginn with stony alarm calls, and with contemptuous ease he drove them off with his axe. Feathers drifted, and the ravens flew shrieking into the pines.

'Birds aren't much use in a fight,' he said scornfully. He seemed to have abandoned all pretence of being human. His clothes were filthy, his scalp scabbed where he'd torn out clumps of hair, his mouth dark with dried blood. 'Where's your wolf?' he sneered. 'Why isn't he rushing to your rescue?'

'You'd like that, wouldn't you?' said Torak, casting about for a weapon. Where *were* Renn and Wolf? Surely they'd heard the commotion? Or was Renn struggling to keep Wolf out of the way?

'Where's your girl?' mocked Naiginn. 'Too frightened to help her mate? Last time I caught her I dragged her after me like a bitch on a leash. I wonder, does she still have the scars?'

Something cold settled inside Torak like a stone. He no longer felt the mud beneath his boots or the heat rising from the pool. He was conscious only of the black pits of the ice demon's gaze – and the blazing urge to kill.

'Let's finish this, Naiginn,' he said levelly. 'We're not in the Deep Forest now, you haven't got a whole clan to back you up, it's just you and me.' Wading into the pool, he beckoned to the ice demon. 'Come and get me.'

Naiginn blinked. He hadn't expected that.

'What's the matter?' jeered Torak. 'Don't like the smell? Does the stink of bloodstone remind you of the Otherworld, where you belong?'

Naiginn drew back his arm and hurled his harpoon. Torak ducked, the shot went wide, the harpoon stuck quivering in mud.

Naiginn took a step into the pool. Grimacing, he plucked a leech from his flank.

'Surely you're not afraid of leeches?' taunted Torak.

'I'm not afraid of anything!' retorted Naiginn.

'Did you know their bite numbs your flesh so you can't feel them on you? Keeps the blood flowing too.' Torak nodded at the scarlet rivulets streaming down his enemy's chest. 'Funny how the smallest creatures can be the worst. Oh, look, three more on your back!'

Naiginn snorted. 'You think I'll fall for that?' He took another step and sank knee-deep, flailing his arms.

'Splashing draws them,' warned Torak. 'And they swim fast, didn't you know?' Groping behind him, his fingers found a rock. He threw it with all his might, hitting the ice demon on the shoulder.

Seizing another rock, Torak flung himself at Naiginn and knocked him backwards into the mud. Now Torak was straddling him, Naiginn putting up his arms to shield his head. Torak's rock struck his forearm, Naiginn dropped his knife with a hiss, but as Torak lunged for it Naiginn flipped him over. They were rolling in and out of the water, Torak battling to wrench the axe from Naiginn's grip. He couldn't do it, sank his teeth into the ice demon's wrist. Naiginn howled and the axe went flying into the ferns.

But already he was on his feet again, ripping a rock the size of his head from the moss and spinning round to smash Torak's skull. Torak hooked one foot round Naiginn's knee and sent him crashing into the pool.

Again they were locked together, Naiginn trying to gouge out Torak's eyes, Torak twisting sideways and kneeing Naiginn in the groin. Naiginn grabbed Torak's hair and forced his head underwater. Torak's blood was roaring in his ears, his sight darkening...

With a desperate heave he flung Naiginn off, seized the ice demon's hair and ground his face into the mud, groping with his free hand for a weapon, but finding nothing, only crumbly deadwood and leech-infested ferns...

Leeches.

Naiginn tore loose and fell on him again. Torak scooped a squirming fistful of leeches and clapped them to the ice demon's face.

Bellowing and clawing his cheeks, Naiginn floundered out of the pool. Torak splashed after him – but the mud was sucking his boots, and in a heartbeat Naiginn had retrieved his axe. Torak couldn't pull free of the mud. Nothing in reach for a weapon.

Out of nowhere, something whistled past his head and hit Naiginn smack on the breastbone. Wide-eyed with shock, the ice demon swayed. Where had that come from?

Another stone hit him on the temple, another on the collarbone. One after another, missiles were pelting down from the slope above, now from one side, now from another.

'We've got you outnumbered!' yelled Renn from somewhere among the trees. 'You can't fight me and Torak *and* the Kelps!'

Bellowing with fury at his unseen attackers, Naiginn scrabbled for his weapons and fled down the slope.

Torak heaved himself out of the mud and stumbled after him, but a stone struck him painfully on the thigh and he fell with a yelp. As he got to his feet another stone hit him in the small of the back.

'Torak, it's over!' called Renn.

Making her way to the pool, she thrust her slingshot into her belt. 'He's gone,' she panted. 'Wolf's safe – at least, for now. That's all that matters!'

TWENTY-ONE

'My one chance and you ruined it!' shouted Torak.

'And I'd do it again in a heartbeat!' said Renn.

He got to his feet and winced. 'Ow. You didn't have to hit me twice.'

'Oh, come on, it's only a bruise.'

'You didn't know that when you chucked those stones.'

'Actually, Torak, I did. In case you've forgotten I'm a pretty good shot with a bow and arrow, and I know what I'm doing with a slingshot. Anyway you should be *thanking* me! I saved Wolf, *and* I stopped you killing Naiginn and being outcast for ever!'

He blew out a long breath, and looked suddenly more

like himself. Not some bare-chested, wild-eyed madman she barely recognized.

'Where is Wolf, anyway?' he muttered, flicking a leech off his breastbone.

'I lured him into that cave with a herring and shut him in with a rock.'

Pulling a face, he put his weight on his bruised leg. 'And I suppose there never were any Kelps throwing stones?'

'Of course not, only me. But Naiginn didn't know that.'

'At least he hasn't got much of a lead.'

Renn didn't reply. She was re-living the moments after she'd shut Wolf in the cave. Frantically filling the lap of her parka with sink-stones and staggering down the slope, stumbling, pebbles spilling into the moss... The terror when she'd realized that the shouting had stopped. The nightmarish sight of Naiginn holding Torak's head underwater...

'You do know that I'm going after him,' said Torak.

She met his eyes. 'You won't catch him.'

'We'll see about that.'

She helped him wash, then flicked the leeches off his back. After that he pulled on his jerkin and parka and they retrieved his weapons from the ferns.

But when they got back to the Ancestors' camp, Wolf was gone. He'd dug himself out of the cave.

Torak howled for him, but there was no reply.

'Surely he won't have gone after Naiginn when you warned him not to?' Renn said in dismay.

'So why doesn't he howl back?' Torak said tersely.

They both knew why. Because a wolf doesn't howl when he's hunting.

'Let's go,' said Torak, shouldering his sleeping-sack. 'At least the tracks will be fresh.'

They were. The moss showed every print of boot and paw, and it was horribly plain that Wolf had indeed gone after Naiginn.

This is my fault, thought Renn. I let Naiginn get away. If he kills Wolf, Torak will never forgive me.

The afternoon wore on and as the light was beginning to fail they caught the sound of the Sea. Then the trees ended and they found themselves following the trails of Naiginn and Wolf onto a narrow shingle beach. The Sea was thinly covered in ice rising and falling on the swell. A line of broken shards leading towards the skyline showed where Naiginn's skinboat had knifed through it.

'Your eyes are better than mine,' said Torak. 'Can you see him?'

Renn squinted. 'There.' She pointed at a distant speck which she could just recognize as a skinboat.

'Has he got Wolf?' Torak said tautly.

'I can't tell, he's too far away.' She pictured Wolf with an arrow in his flank, slumped unconscious in Naiginn's boat.

Torak had left her and was moving along the beach, head down, reading his pack-brother's trail. His fists were clenched as he walked slowly along the shore, then back again. Now he was turning inland, following a small creek that tumbled over the rocks.

Suddenly he beckoned to her. 'It's allright!' he shouted. 'Wolf got here *after* Naiginn had left! He headed up this creek, back into the Forest!' Putting his hands to his mouth, he howled.

Still no reply. But this time, Torak broke into a grin. 'He's probably sulking because you shut him in that cave!'

Wolf was *furious* with the pack-sister for shutting him in that cave. It had been awful hearing Tall Tailless fighting the demon and being unable to help. And he'd broken a claw digging himself out.

Tall Tailless and the pack-sister had been so busy squabbling they hadn't noticed him go, but by the time he'd reached the shore he was too late, the demon was escaping over the Great Wet.

Mewing in frustration, Wolf had headed back into the Forest up a steep little Fast Wet. Now as he flew along its rocky banks, he wondered *why* the pack-sister had shut him in. Had she been trying to stop him attacking the demon?

Tall Tailless had also told him not to go after the demon – but *why*? The pale-pelt was the fiercest, cruellest demon Wolf had ever encountered. Tall Tailless and the pack-sister couldn't fight it on their own. They *needed* Wolf.

Tall Tailless's howl drifted on the wind. *Where – are – you?*

Leaping onto a log, Wolf was about to howl back when the wind changed, swamping him in the strong fishy smell of the taillesses who'd trapped him. His pelt tightened with alarm. Surely he wasn't anywhere near their Den?

He stood snuffing, twitching his ears to catch the sounds. Many taillesses were crashing through the Forest, their dogs panting, claws clicking on rocks as they snuffled for his scent.

Wolf went hurtling up the slope.

The taillesses were shouting, their dogs barking furiously: they'd caught his scent.

Fallen trees rolled beneath Wolf's paws and he scrambled over stones slimy with moss. The way ahead grew narrower and steeper. The Fast Wet was roaring in his ears, drenching him with spray.

Wolf skittered to a halt. Above him the Fast Wet came thundering down a cliff. On either side loomed unclimbable boulders like jaws waiting to snap. Wolf couldn't find a way through.

He was trapped.

'You were our guests – and you deceived us!' Chinoot glared at his captives as he paced the platform overlooking Wolf's pen. 'You fled from us and you took our wolf!'

'He's not your wolf,' growled Torak.

Renn elbowed him to be quiet. 'We didn't take him,' she told the Leader. 'He was gone when we reached his pen, we *had* to go after him to save him from the demon!'

'So you *say*,' snarled Chinoot.

Night had fallen, and torchlight glinted on the great white tooth on the Leader's breast. His narrow red features were rigid with fury. It made no difference that Torak and Renn had given themselves up the moment they'd learnt that Wolf had been recaptured.

The Kelps crowded about the platform, muttering angrily. Halut, Elupalee and Lathren stared stonily at the captives, while Yamna huddled against her mother, looking terrified: she was the one who'd set Wolf free.

Renn caught her eye and shook her head: *I won't tell on you.*

'Even *if* what you say is true,' Chinoot went on, 'that demon is no longer a threat. My scouts saw him in his skinboat heading east.'

'He'll be back,' said Renn.

'He'll regret it if he tries!' Chinoot struck the platform twice with his staff. 'It is settled. You and the wolf remain with us.'

'And Wolf is miserable for the rest of his life!' burst out Torak. 'Look at him pacing! You know he won't eat!'

Chinoot folded his arms on his chest. 'He will when he's hungry.'

'Is that how you honour him?' cried Torak.

'There's something you haven't thought of,' said Renn.

'Keeping Wolf against his will can't possibly please the Ancestors—'

'Who are you to talk of the Ancestors?' shrilled Lathren.

'Look what those ravens are doing!' broke in Halut. 'That proves the Ancestors are angry!'

All heads turned to where Rip and Rek were stalking about, flipping over the clam shells that bordered the path to Wolf's pen and flinging them this way and that.

'Ravens carry messages from the Ancient Ones,' said Chinoot, fingering his tassel of grey human hair. 'Halut's right: the Ancestors are angry.'

'But not with us,' put in Torak. 'While we were in the Forest, your Ancestors led us to their camp.'

Renn shot him a glance. *Good idea.* 'They sent me a vision,' she told Chinoot. Briefly she described what she'd seen, omitting only what the Ancestor woman had told her, as she had a feeling that those words were meant for her alone.

Some of the Kelps were impressed, but Chinoot's brow-spots rose in disbelief. 'More lies! Why would the Ancestors honour strangers who flout our hospitality? Who smear the fine clothes we gave them with mud?'

'I don't know, but they did,' insisted Renn. 'Here's proof!' From her medicine pouch she drew the egg-shaped sink-stone and held it out.

The Kelp Leader took it and turned it in his fingers. He handed it back. 'So?'

Renn had an idea. 'You celebrate Egg Dawn, don't you?'

'Of course. But what—'

'Remember I told you that Wolf's mate is due to have cubs any day now? What if this stone egg is a sign? What if the Ancestors want Wolf to be back with his mate by Egg Dawn?'

Doubtful murmurs among the crowd. Again Chinoot fingered his tassel. Suddenly his face cleared. 'Maybe part of what you say is right, and you do have the Ancient Ones' favour – but you're wrong about what it means. It means they want you to stay here and celebrate Egg Dawn with us.'

Torak flung up his arms. 'Renn, this is hopeless, we're getting nowhere!'

She didn't reply. The answer had come to her in a flash.

The most powerful impression she'd gained from her vision in the Forest was the Ancestors' closeness to each other: the dense web of friendship and affection in which they'd lived their lives. It was the same for their descendants. What mattered most to the Kelps was kinship.

She turned to Torak. 'We've been making this too complicated.'

'What do you mean?'

'I think,' she said in a low voice, 'I know what we have to do.'

Torak dropped into the pen, and Wolf stopped pacing and looked at him dully. He padded over to his pack-brother and gave him a listless nose-nudge, then slumped down and put his muzzle between his paws.

Ignoring the throng watching on the platform, Torak squatted beside him and said in wolf talk: *You're sad.*

Wolf's whiskers twitched. *I miss Darkfur. And Pebble and the others.*

The pack-sister, said Torak, *knows a way to make the taillesses set us free.*

Wolf's eyes slid to Renn, standing a few paces away, then back to Torak. *How?*

Howl for Darkfur and the others.

Wolf heaved a sigh. *They're too far away, they can't hear.*

Pack-brother, you need to do this!

Wolf's amber eyes grazed his in puzzlement.

Trust me, said Torak. *Howl to them! Tell them how much you miss them!*

For a moment Wolf lay still. Then he heaved himself to his feet and padded a few steps. He glanced back at Torak. Then he put up his muzzle and howled.

At first his howls were low and tentative, but they soon gathered force as his feelings welled to the surface.

On the platform people shook their heads in wonder, and put their hands to their mouths and blinked back tears. Wolf's howls were full of pain and longing: the purest and saddest of songs. Again and again he sent his loneliness winging through the night – until at last his howls sank to a long, plaintive note that died away to silence.

He stood with drooping head and tail. Then he slumped onto his side and shut his eyes.

Nobody broke the silence. Torches crackled. The Sea surged and sucked at the shore.

A voice spoke brokenly. 'I know how the wolf feels.' It was Halut. 'I felt the same after the Thunderstar struck. My brothers and I were trapped among strangers. We couldn't get back to the Island. It's the worst feeling of all, to be cut off from your clan.'

Others were murmuring agreement. Only Chinoot was scowling. Yamna's cheeks were wet with tears. 'He sounded so lonely.'

'He *is* lonely,' said Torak. 'He has Renn and me, but it's not enough, he misses his mate.' He and Renn approached the platform and stared up at Chinoot. 'Wolves mate for life,' Torak went on. 'He'll never get over losing Darkfur.'

'If you keep him here,' said Renn, 'then no matter how well you care for him, he will be lonely and miserable for ever.'

Chinoot's scowl deepened. He cleared his throat. 'That can't be the will of the Ancestors,' he said at last. Once more he rapped twice with his staff. 'My decision is made. We have to let the wolf go.'

TWENTY-TWO

'Remember,' said Kujai. 'Twist *away* from the target, then towards – *then* let go.'

Dark managed the twisting bit, but when he cast the net it spread out in a ragged crescent and flopped messily into the river.

'Better,' said Kujai, drawing in his own net, which had floated onto the water in a perfect circle.

'Better isn't good enough,' growled Dark. 'Not for catching the souls of a demon.'

'Try again. And remember to cast *up*wards.'

For the hundredth time Dark went through the steps

which he still had to think about, but which came to Kujai as naturally as breathing. Grasp the gathered net in one hand, loop the handline round your wrist; take one of the weights and drape that part of the net over your shoulder; hold half of what's left in your free hand, swing backwards, then forwards – and cast.

This time it was slightly better, but when he tried to pull in the net it wouldn't come.

'It's snagged on something,' said Kujai.

'I can see that,' snapped Dark, wading in to retrieve it.

The net was tangled on a submerged stump. Angrily he tried to cut it free with his knife, and only succeeded in snapping a flint. With a roar he flung the weapon at the bank, startling Ark, who flew off with a squawk.

Kujai folded his arms and hacked at the snow with his heel. Among the ice floes a flock of eider ducks made a noise a lot like laughter.

Dark plunged his hand into the freezing water and the net unhooked itself. Feeling foolish, he waded back to the bank. He was cold and wet and he'd eaten nothing since the night before, except for a nasty purifying mash of betony and hedge-mustard. He would have to skip nightmeal too: no food till he'd made the Egg Offering.

'Did you damage the net?' said Kujai.

He shook his head.

'Good. Let's try again.'

Dark drew a breath. 'This isn't going to work.'

'Yes, it is, you're much better than when you started.'

'Kujai. You've been casting nets all your life, you do it without thinking. It'll take me ages to reach that point!'

'Then let me do it for you! When – if – the demon comes, you throw the spear and I'll cast the—'

'I've told you, you *can't*! It has to be a Mage!'

'So we'll get Watash to do it, she knows how—' He broke off with a frown. Three days before, the Sea-eagle Mage had slipped and broken her wrist. 'Another Mage, then. The Willows or the Vipers—'

'It'd take days to fetch them and we don't have days! It's going to be soon. I can feel it.'

'How soon?'

'I wish I knew.'

They'd been practising on a stretch of the Elk River downstream from the Raven camp, at one of the few patches of open water.

Tonight the Moon of Roaring Rivers would be full. By now every river in the Forest should be a noisy tumult of jostling floes and debris swept down from upstream; but not this winter. Only last night had the wind finally changed and the thaw set in. Even now the Elk River seemed reluctant to wake, the ice scarcely moving on the black water.

The Forest felt tense, waiting for the chaos of spring to erupt. All along the frozen rivers the clans had planted spears on the ice in readiness: when a spear tilted, they would know the river was beginning to wake. And if a storm in the Mountains sent a surge of meltwater that risked a flood, they had hollow logs ready for drumming the alarm...

Ice clinked in the shallows at Dark's feet. His stomach tightened. While his mind had been elsewhere, a floe had glided stealthily in. That's how Naiginn will return, he thought. I won't even know till it's too late.

The long blue twilight was coming on: the demon time. For days Dark had been sensing lesser demons creeping out of the ice. Lurking in shadows, willing him to fail. They knew Naiginn was coming.

Wordlessly, he shook out the sodden net and laid it in the snow to dry. He slumped onto a boulder.

Tomorrow was Egg Dawn, the time of greatest change. A dangerous time, when darkness and light are evenly matched: when the world teeters on a knife edge between winter and spring, good and evil, life and death.

The slightest feather-touch could tilt the balance. To help it towards the good, Mages everywhere would be making the Egg Offering. Before daybreak Dark would climb the ridge above camp and offer crossbill eggs in a nest of mistletoe lined with eagle down.

But how could he do that *and* keep watch for Naiginn?

Kujai sat beside him, making him jump. 'I'm on edge too,' said the Sea-eagle boy. 'We all are. It's just the thaw.'

'It's more than that,' said Dark.

'Tell me.'

Dark studied his square, capable face; the strawberry stain on his cheek. Kujai knew all about fishing and canoes, but he wasn't a Mage and he couldn't see ghosts. How could he possibly understand?

'Tell me,' urged Kujai.

Dark hesitated. 'They come out of the ice,' he said. 'Lesser demons – the Walker calls them slinkers and scurriers. More of them than I've sensed since just after the Thunderstar. I think they know their master is coming.' With a stick he dug at the snow. 'And there's something else.'

Kujai waited.

'Last night after moonrise, Ark flew into our shelter. She circled the roofpost three times, then flew out again. Kujai, she's never done that before – and I don't know what it means! I only know it's bad.'

'How do you know? How do you "sense" these things?'

Dark sighed. 'It's like... you know when you're in a boat and you glance over the side? One moment you're looking at your name-soul on the water. Then you shift your gaze and you're looking *into* it, at seaweed and fishes. Like that. A different way of seeing.'

Kujai was nodding. 'A bit like being out at Sea and sensing a change in the weather.'

'A bit,' said Dark.

They exchanged tentative smiles.

Footsteps in the snow, and they turned to see Fin-Kedinn limping towards them, his old dog Grip walking stiffly at his heels.

They rose, and the Raven Leader eased himself onto their boulder, stretching out his bad leg with a wince. Ark perched in a nearby alder, spiking her head-feathers and glaring at Grip. The dog growled at her, but a word from Fin-Kedinn silenced him.

'Seems you chipped your knife,' said the Raven Leader, holding up Dark's weapon which he'd retrieved from the bank.

'I lost my temper,' muttered Dark.

To his surprise, instead of returning the knife, Fin-Kedinn offered his own. 'I'll mend yours, we'll swap later. How's the practice going?'

'Very well,' said Kujai.

'Awful,' said Dark at the same time.

Fin-Kedinn's mouth twitched. 'Which?'

'I have to be able to cast without thinking and I'm nowhere near,' said Dark.

Fin-Kedinn considered that. 'Kujai, will you leave us? I need to speak to my Mage alone.'

'Of course.' Kujai shot Dark a glance and raised his eyebrows: *Wonder what it's about?*

Fin-Kedinn waited till he was out of earshot, then asked Dark to cast the net again. Dark was reluctantly preparing to throw when Ark suddenly did something extraordinary. She swooped onto the boulder beside Fin-Kedinn and bowed to him.

Dark was astonished. The white raven was supremely wary, she never approached anyone but him.

The Raven Leader sat very still, never taking his eyes off Ark. She hopped onto his wrist, then sidled up his forearm. Slowly, Fin-Kedinn raised his arm. Ark tilted back her head and met his gaze. Then, with a low, throaty aah! she flew off into the trees.

Fin-Kedinn's features were like granite as he watched her go.

Grip, who'd backed away with hackles raised, shook himself and returned to his master's side.

'She's never done that before,' Dark said in a low voice.

'Has she not?' Fin-Kedinn said remotely. Clearing his throat, he came back to himself with an effort. Then he drew something from a pouch at his belt. 'I'd like you to take this.' He held out Torak's medicine horn.

'Why?' Dark said uneasily.

'For safe-keeping.'

'If you want me to, but—'

'Now show me the weapons you've made.' His tone warned Dark that the subject was closed.

Kujai had helped Dark weave the net, using strong twine of twisted kelp and making the mesh very fine, so that the ice demon's souls couldn't slip through. For weights Dark had tied his little stone creatures around the rim.

'It's a good net,' said Fin-Kedinn, setting it down.

'But it's missing the vital thing. I've nothing of Naiginn's to bind his souls.'

'Show me the spear.'

Dark fetched it from where he'd propped it against the alder. He was proud of it. He might not be able to cast nets, but he knew about spears. This one had a sturdy ash shaft and a barbed head of red deer antler stained with purple earthblood. He'd twisted one of his precious mammut hairs around the socket to give it the strength of the Deep Past.

A spear to kill and a net to bind… He tried to shut his mind to the fact that his purpose was to kill.

What if I can't do it? he thought in sudden panic. What if I hesitate and miss my chance?

Fin-Kedinn hefted the spear to his shoulder, closed one eye and peered along the shaft. 'It's a good spear,' he said, handing it back.

'It's missing the same thing as the net: something of Naiginn's.'

The Raven Leader's blue eyes pierced his. 'Dark,' he said quietly. 'You can't do this.'

'I have to.'

'You said yourself, you're not good enough with the net.'

'You think I'm going to fail.'

'I don't think killing Naiginn is for you to do.'

Dark marched down to the river and stared at the ice.

'Are you still sure that Naiginn will come back?' Fin-Kedinn called after him.

'Oh, yes, I'm sure,' he said over his shoulder.

'When?'

'Soon.'

'Then I'll post scouts on the Point to keep watch.'

'You can, but I think he'll slip through.'

'What about Torak and Renn?' Fin-Kedinn's voice was sharp with concern. 'What do the signs tell you?'

'They're coming too,' said Dark. 'They're all coming. Here, to this valley, like ravens to a kill.'

As he walked back to Fin-Kedinn, something crunched beneath his foot. He bent and picked it up. It was the remains of an eider duck egg, broken and pecked clean.

Eggs, he thought. He looked at Fin-Kedinn. 'Tomorrow,' he said in an altered voice. 'Egg Dawn. That's when it will be.'

TWENTY-THREE

S till dark, although daybreak wasn't far off. 'Egg Dawn,'
muttered Renn, rolling up her sleeping-sack. 'I can't
wait to get back to the Forest.'

'Me too,' said Torak. 'I just wish we could've got there
yesterday.'

With the Kelps guiding them they'd hoped to reach
the coast in a single day, but icebergs and a fierce east
wind had slowed them down, forcing them to put in for
the night on this bleak little islet in the middle of the
Sea. Only Yamna had been pleased. Having begged to
be allowed to come, she was desperate to put off saying
goodbye to Wolf.

'Where's Wolf gone?' said Renn.

'He went after eider ducks.'

'D'you think you'll have trouble with him again?'

'I hope not.' After Wolf's ordeal on the iceberg it had taken them ages to coax him into a boat.

With the moon full, they had no need of torches as they righted their canoe, which they'd been using as a shelter. Two of the Kelps' big ten-man crafts were already in the shallows and Chinoot's men were hoisting the third on their shoulders.

Once he'd made his decision, preparations for the crossing had been swift. It turned out that his people had already repaired Kujai's canoe (no sense wasting a good boat); and they'd also returned Torak and Renn's own clothes and weapons. Renn was mightily relieved to be back in her old reindeer hides, which still smelt of the Forest, and it was reassuring to see Torak looking more like himself.

She watched Chinoot place a piece of halibut liver on the blade of his paddle and tip it into the shallows as an offering to the Sea Mother. Raising his arms, he prayed to the glowing green waves in the sky, which he said were a vast Forest of kelp. Renn saw one luminous branch of the First Tree break in two, then fade into the stars. She didn't know what it meant, but it made her uneasy.

'The Kelp Forest in the Sky foretells trouble,' Chinoot said in a low voice.

'What kind of trouble?' she said.

'Hard to say. Maybe bad weather. Maybe worse.'

She considered that. 'My clan is camped on the Elk River. When we get near the coast, will you be able to point us in the right direction?'

The Leader's inlaid fangs gleamed. 'Of course! We may not often visit the East, but we know our way around the coast!'

Torak was already waiting, the canoe rocking on the swell. As Renn climbed aboard she saw Wolf emerge from the gloom and come racing over the shingle, his dislike of boats forgotten in his eagerness not to be left behind.

A small forlorn figure scrambled out of Chinoot's boat and ran towards him, wailing. It was Yamna. Wolf turned aside and gave her a quick farewell lick, then splashed into the shallows and leapt for the canoe, landing in a heap on Renn.

Yamna stood on the shingle, hiccupping with grief.

'Wait,' muttered Torak. Vaulting over the side, he waded back to Yamna, then took the little slate wolf from his neck and put it round hers. 'That's for saving Wolf,' he told her. 'When summer comes, maybe your mother will send you to be fostered with the Ravens. Then you'll see him again.'

The child sniffed and nodded and clutched the stone wolf.

Chinoot was calling her name, and she hurried back to the canoes.

'That was a good thing you did,' Renn told Torak

when he'd taken his place in the boat. He didn't reply, and she wasn't sure if he'd heard. As they got under way she thought about the different Toraks she'd seen over the past few days: the wild-eyed killer who'd attacked Naiginn with alarming savagery, and the boy she loved, who'd just been kind to an unhappy little girl.

The wind was in the west and they made good speed, Torak paddling in the bow, Renn paddling in the stern, and occasionally grabbing the steering-oar to steer around icebergs. Wolf huddled between them, panting and drooling and being sick.

For a while gulls followed them, hoping for fish. Then a pod of Sea wolves appeared and raced them, before pulling ahead and vanishing into the spray. Torak cast them a wistful glance. As the sky grew lighter, Renn quickened her strokes. Now that they were almost home, her need to see Fin-Kedinn was an ache in her chest.

Suddenly Wolf sprang to his feet, making the canoe rock wildly. Torak growled at him to get down, but Wolf ignored him. His tail was high, his ears rammed forwards. He was staring ahead, snuffing the air.

Soon afterwards Renn glimpsed a scarlet thread on the skyline, and beneath it a spiky black line.

Torak let out a whoop and threw his paddle in the air. *'The Forest!'*

Already Chinoot was bringing his canoe about and ordering the other Kelp crafts to do the same. 'That's Elk River ahead!' he called. 'May your Ancestors protect you – and watch out for Sea ice, going in!' Waving away their thanks, he and his band dug in their paddles and went flying over the waves. Soon Torak and Renn were left alone.

As they paddled closer, the Forest rose steadily out of the Sea, and they spotted the twin headlands at the mouth of Elk River. Above it the sky was wolf grey, slashed with ominous crimson.

Renn slipped her hand under her gutskin over-parka and touched her ravenbeak amulet. A red sky on a normal morning meant bad weather. What, she wondered, did it portend on Egg Dawn?

'Ice ahead!' shouted Torak.

Seizing the steering-oar, she steered them round an island of pale-green ice lurking just beneath the surface. They exchanged glances. Ice was Naiginn's element.

'First the icebergs on the crossing,' said Torak. 'Now this. Feels as if it's helping him.'

The instant they passed into the shelter of the headlands, the wind dropped to nothing and the waves smoothed out. The thaw had begun, and Elk River was choked with drift ice: they found themselves winding their way through narrow channels of black water between the floes. On either side the valley walls rose steeply, the pines dark and silent against the snow. Renn couldn't see the Sea-eagle camp on the south bank, and she remembered that they often moved upstream after the herring run, to shelter from the spring storms.

Ice bumped against the boat. Torak fended it off with his paddle. 'D'you think Naiginn's already here?' he said quietly.

She nodded. 'He's had two days' lead. And he knows we'll come back to this valley because it's where the pack is.'

The long shivering cry of a diverbird broke the stillness. Another sign of bad weather to come.

As they paddled upstream, Renn became aware of an ugly pressure in her chest. Twice from the corner of her eye she glimpsed shadows slipping behind the trees on the bank. Wolf stood stiffly, his hackles bristling. Lowering his head, he growled.

'Demons,' said Torak.

Renn nodded. 'Perhaps they're coming to his call.'

They passed a flock of eider ducks bobbing on the water. She thought, If I had a bow I could shoot one as easily as looking at it. That's how easy it will be for Naiginn to shoot us if he's watching from the bank.

'We should keep to the midstream,' Torak said over his shoulder.

'Yes,' she said, taking the steering-oar. 'Out of arrowshot.'

The Demon watches the canoe veer out of arrowshot, and lowers its bow.

No matter. They tried to evade it before by hiding among those weaklings the Kelps, but they've only postponed the inevitable. Nothing can keep the Demon from its prey.

Scornfully it watches the boy and girl labouring among the floes. They don't know it yet, but further upstream a great mountain of ice has seized the river by the neck, throttling it into submission.

And now the Demon smells more ice on the way: this time it will come from the sky. Ice always wins, the Demon gloats. Nothing can beat me now!

The Demon has enjoyed itself on the north bank, outwitting the mortals camped there, savaging trees, feeding at will on the creatures of the Forest. Bird, fawn, human – it doesn't matter, so long as the Demon can feed. But the souls are weak, merely sharpening its hunger, and now it has returned to the south bank, where there are no mortals. Soon it will lure the quarry here and make the kill.

Shouldering its weapons, the Demon slides along the bank on its snow-skates, leaving the boy and girl toiling on the river. Shadows slither and scurry in its wake. The lesser demons are eager to do its will.

Suddenly the Demon catches the smell of the wolf's souls on the wind, and its hunger flares agonizingly strong. Soon, it tells itself, those bright souls will be mine. Nothing can stop me: not the girl, not the boy, not that pallid, feeble Mage or the lame old Raven Leader. All will be crushed and swept aside. I will feast on the wolf's blazing souls – and at last my spirit will burst free of this mortal flesh! Then nothing will stand in my way. I will rule all. I will devour all. I will be stronger than the sun!

As the Demon powers over the snow, deer flee and birds fly screeching into the sky. Trees creak and groan. The Demon hates trees. Especially birches. The black marks on their white trunks are like eyes staring at him. . .

They are eyes, hundreds of them — like the ones near the wolf den. How dare they stare at the Great Demon!

Slewing to a halt, the Demon whips out its axe and hacks at the watching trunks. Cut out the eyes! Slash them till they ooze!

Drunk with destruction, it pauses for breath. It laughs. The trees have given it an idea.

Choosing a beech sapling which will be easily spotted from the river, the Demon draws its knife and carves the boy's Forest mark in its smooth brown skin. Now for the girl's mark, the raven claw. Lastly, the Demon crosses out both marks with its own mark, the Narwal tusk.

'There,' pants the Demon. 'Is that plain enough for you? Come and find me — if you dare!'

'There,' Renn said quietly, pointing at the alder sapling on the bank. 'It's his mark. That's the fifth so far. They're very fresh.'

'He's telling us he's here,' said Torak.

'A challenge. Well, he'll get his wish soon enough.'

'We're veering off course. Steer us back to the midstream.'

Wolf pushed past Torak and stood in the bow, whining impatiently. His eyes were fixed on the opposite bank where the Den was and he was shifting from paw to paw, eager to jump in and swim for it.

Stay with me, pack-brother, Torak warned in wolf talk.

Wolf's glance grazed his, then returned to the bank. Torak hated to see him torn between the need to go to his mate and the desire to remain with his pack-brother.

Not for much longer, he thought. Naiginn was on the south bank, the Den and the Raven camp were on the north. Torak knew what he had to do. He would put in at the north bank just long enough to let Wolf and Renn ashore, then head back across the river and go after Naiginn.

Renn flashed him an edgy grin. 'I can't wait to see Fin-Kedinn!' Her face was flushed, her bright hair aglow in the grey storm light. Torak saw the freckle at the corner of her mouth that he loved. He felt a stab of panic. When he killed Naiginn he would be outcast for ever, and if he tried to see her she would be outcast too, cut off from Fin-Kedinn for the rest of her life. He couldn't do that to her. Which meant that this was the last time he could be with her.

Storm clouds were massing like mountains in the sky, but behind them the sun was strong, the thaw gathering pace. As they glided upriver they heard snow sliding off trees, the noise of meltwater trickling and gurgling. And yet bizarrely, the further they went, the less ice they encountered, and instead of battling a current in spate, Torak could hardly feel it. *Why?* Elk River was the unruly child of the two greatest rivers in the Forest, the Widewater and the Blackwater – who took their strength from the High Mountains themselves. They were at their most dangerous during the thaw. Why, then, was the river so eerily quiet?

Rounding a bend, he had his answer. In the distance where the valley narrowed, the Neck was choked by a chaotic jumble of ice swept down from upstream and now blocking the river.

Ice, he thought in alarm. Always ice.

'I can't see any woodsmoke ahead,' said Renn.

'The Ravens have probably moved to higher ground. When the river breaks through that ice there'll be a flood.'

'Yes, that must be it. Look, there's a place to land over there between those trees!'

Again Torak's spirit quailed. How could he leave her? How could he leave Wolf? Maybe if they all stayed with the Ravens they'd be safe, and Fin-Kedinn and Dark could help them work out what to do about Naiginn...

Wolf, sensing something amiss, leant briefly against him, and Torak slipped off his gauntlet and sank his fingers into his pack-brother's scruff. He took a last sniff of Wolf's beloved scent. He gave him a final nose-nudge. *Go to Darkfur!*

You're coming too, Wolf said distractedly. He'd caught the scent of the Den and was getting ready to leap ashore.

Torak's heart pounded in his ears as he drew nearer the place Renn had indicated, a stretch of flat rocks between overhanging willows. Bringing the canoe alongside, he grabbed a branch to steady it. Wolf leapt onto the bank, his hindquarters briefly sinking in slush; then he heaved himself out and sped off.

'You first,' Torak told Renn. 'I'll pass you your gear and tie up the boat.'

The rocks weren't as steady as they looked and she had to concentrate on not falling in. 'Watch your footing or you'll slip,' she warned.

Wordlessly he handed her her pack. She was turning to go when he pulled her to him and kissed her hard on the mouth.

'What—'

'I'm sorry,' he told her as he pushed off into the river. 'I have to do this alone. Tell Fin-Kedinn I'm sorry too!'

TWENTY-FOUR

The yowls of Tall Tailless and the pack-sister fell away as Wolf loped towards the Den. He sensed that Darkfur's time was near. He had to keep her safe and protect the new cubs who were being born.

Running through the slushy drifts wasn't easy, and he had to keep dodging heaps of Bright Soft Cold falling off trees. The Thunderer was growling in the Up, and Wolf's pelt was prickling as it did before a storm. From further ahead came grinding booms and cracks, where the Fast Wet was fighting the mountain of Bright Hard Cold that was holding it back.

As Wolf neared the Den he smelt tree-blood and heard birches moaning in pain. Worry clawed his guts as he caught the stink of demon. The pale-pelted one had savaged the trees till their hide hung in tatters from their trunks. Wolf sensed the demon's hatred of the Forest, its hunger to destroy. And although its scent wasn't fresh, it had been frighteningly close to the Den.

Where *was* the Den? By now Wolf should be running through a rich stream of welcoming wolf scents – and yet what was flowing over his nose was the cold, threatening smell of Fast Wet.

He lurched to a halt. *What was this?* Instead of the Den, he found himself standing before a sullen expanse of black Wet, clogged with fallen trees and chunks of Bright Hard Cold. Mewing in distress, Wolf ran up and down. But sniff as he might, he could find no scent-marks on the trees, no beloved pack smells on the wind.

In a snap he realized what had happened. The Fast Wet hadn't been able to break through the mountain of Bright Hard Cold – so it had drowned the valley. *It had drowned the Den.*

Suddenly Wolf was a cub again, shivering and alone. Around him in the mud lay his mother and father and pack-mates, sodden and Not-Breath…

Wolf put up his muzzle and howled. Pebble, Blackear, Whitethroat, Darkfur, the new cubs… *All gone.*

Quork!

Wolf broke off in mid-howl.

Quork-quork! Both ravens landed in front of him and hopped about, cawing urgently.

Wolf snarled and they flew to the nearest pine, where they peered at him with bright excited eyes. Why couldn't they leave him alone?

Hitching their wings, the birds flew off, heading uphill and waggling their tail feathers, as they did when they wanted him to follow.

Now they were returning and swooping over him, now flying off again, still waggling their tails.

But they were no long cawing. Instead they were *whining*. Whining like wolf cubs demanding to be fed.

Renn, standing before what remained of the Ravens' camp, heard Wolf's howls abruptly cut off.

Terrible images flashed through her mind: Wolf felled by a poisoned arrow, alive but unable to move... Naiginn bending over him to feed...

Torak would have known why Wolf had howled and what he was saying. If only Torak was with her now. And yet she couldn't be angry with him for leaving her and going to hunt Naiginn on his own. She'd been planning to do the same thing as soon as she could get her hands on a bow.

Setting her pack on the ground, she eased her shoulders. Storm clouds were darkening the sky, the pines soughing in the rising wind. From upstream came grinding cracks and groans as the river fought to break free of the ice.

The Ravens had abandoned camp in a hurry, tearing down part of their winter shelter to make it easier to remove their gear. Inside, what had been a snug sleeping platform strewn with reindeer pelts was now a mess of muddy brushwood. In the ashes of the firepit Renn found a child's toy auroch of plaited bark, forgotten in the rush.

A swathe of trampled snow leading uphill told her that Torak had guessed right, and the clan had moved to higher ground. She faced a long steep trudge through slushy drifts to find them – and she didn't have snowshoes.

A birch-bark horn rang out, two long blasts echoing across the valley. Fin-Kedinn was sounding the alarm, summoning all remaining hunters to rejoin the clan.

Suddenly Renn heard the scrape of runners, the patter of paws, and Kujai came rattling down the slope on a two-man sled drawn by four sturdy dogs.

He spotted Renn and slewed to a halt. No time for greetings: 'Fin-Kedinn sent me to pick up stragglers!' he panted.

'Where is he?' she cried eagerly.

'He went to find Dark!' His brow creased with worry. 'He climbed the ridge before daybreak to make the Egg Offering, should've been back by now. Where's Torak?'

'Other side of the river.'

'Well, he'd better get to high ground fast! My clan's

camped further inland, they've been drumming flood warnings all night, didn't you hear?'

'No, we only reached the coast this morning—'

'Ice is blocking the Neck, but 'meltwater's surging downstream. It can't hold much longer, that's why Fin-Kedinn gave the order to break camp!'

'Where have they gone?'

Stooping to check the dogs' traces, he pointed at the ridge. 'They're racing to build new shelters before the storm breaks. Jump on the sled, we've got to get out of here!'

She was shouldering her pack when someone shouted Kujai's name from the slope and the Sea-eagle boy's face lit up. *'Dark!'*

Dark's tall thin form emerged from the pines and hurried downhill as fast as his snowshoes would allow. He was carrying a spear and had a net over one shoulder. Behind him came another man, also armed, but moving more slowly and leaning on a staff. Fin-Kedinn hadn't yet seen Renn, the remains of the shelter were in the way. 'We heard voices!' he called to Kujai.

'He was talking to me,' she said shakily.

Her uncle saw her and went still. *'Renn!'*

Then she was running to him and he was holding her so tight she couldn't breathe, and she was burying her head in his smoky-smelling parka as she used to do when she was a child.

Gripping her shoulders, he held her at arm's length and searched her face. 'I prayed I'd see you one more time.'

She was shocked at how gaunt he'd become, his blue eyes bloodshot and shadowed with pain.

'Where's Torak?' he said.

'Across the river, he's gone after Naiginn.' Briefly she told them about the marks they'd seen on the trees.

The Raven Leader exchanged glances with Dark. 'Dark spotted the demon from the ridge.'

'Where was he heading?' she demanded.

'I don't know,' said Dark, 'I only saw him for a moment.'

'We'll find him,' said Fin-Kedinn. 'There's a boat moored not far from here—'

'I'm coming too!' Renn broke in. 'Dark, where's my bow?'

'Up at the camp, I left it with Thull—'

'Fin-Kedinn, lend me your bow!'

To her consternation he shook his head. 'No, Renn. This demon will not be killed by any bow.'

'Maybe not, but I can slow him down – and you know I'm the best shot here!'

'We have better weapons,' put in Dark. 'Look: a spear to kill, and a net to bind!'

That brought her up short. 'A *net*! Why didn't I think of that?'

'D'you know how to cast it?' said Dark.

'Of course.'

'Then take it. But it's missing something: I have nothing to bind it to Naiginn.'

'I do!' Wrenching open her medicine pouch, she pulled out the demon's long fair hairs.

'Is that good?' put in Kujai, watching Dark's face.

'Oh, yes!' Dark said with feeling. Then to Renn: 'I'll wind one round the spear, you do the net.'

'You can do both on the way to the boat,' said Fin-Kedinn. 'Kujai, we're taking your sled. Renn, you go with him up to the new camp—'

'*No!*' she cried.

Fin-Kedinn's face went hard. 'That's an order, Renn.'

'I am not skulking in camp while you're in danger! You know it makes sense for me to go with you, I'm the best shot in the Forest!'

'You are a Mage! Act like one!' Her uncle's sternness made her flinch. 'If Dark doesn't return from this, your clan will need you as never before!'

'What about Torak?' she flung back. 'Doesn't he need me? He's all alone on the other side of the river, battling an *ice demon!* Don't you even *care?*'

'Wait!' broke in Dark. 'I think we're getting this wrong!'

'What do you mean?' said Renn.

'What if Naiginn isn't on the other side? What if those marks on the trees were a trick, and he's crossed to *this* side without us knowing?'

'Why would he do that?' said Renn.

'Remember the trick he played on you and Torak the day Wolf was swept away? What if he's doing it again? Leaving marks in plain sight as a decoy—'

'—*while he goes after Wolf!*' cried Renn. 'Oh, Dark, you're right, Naiginn knows Wolf will make straight for the Den!'

She turned to Fin-Kedinn. 'He's waiting for Wolf right now! Maybe he's already shot him! The Den's just round that bend, let's go!'

'You won't reach it in the sled, the ground's too rough,' said Kujai.

'Then we'll go on foot,' said Dark.

Renn pleaded with her uncle. '*Please*, you have to let us go!'

For a heartbeat he looked at her. Then he nodded. 'Dark, take the spear. Renn, you have the net. Kujai and I will take the sled back to camp.'

Kujai opened his mouth to protest, but the Raven Leader quelled him with a glance, then turned back to Renn. 'The drifts are deep. Here, have my snowshoes.'

Swiftly she tied them on. Then she and Dark started uphill. They hadn't gone far when something made her glance back.

Fin-Kedinn stood by the sled watching them go, a strange wistful expression on his face.

'What I said about Torak,' she called down to him. 'I didn't mean it, I know you care!'

The hard features softened. 'Too many demons about, trying to make us fight!' Putting his fist to his breast, he raised his staff to her in blessing. 'You be careful up there. And, Renn... May the guardian fly with you!'

TWENTY-FIVE

The Demon watches in fury as the canoe reaches the other side of the river and the wolf leaps ashore and disappears into the trees. This should not be happening! Why haven't they taken the bait and come here, where the Demon is waiting?

Savagely it hacks a sapling to pieces and snaps up its bewildered spirit. It raises its axe to destroy another — it lowers it with a hiss.

No more hiding in shadows. No more feeding on insignificant little souls! Only the spirit of the wolf can satisfy the Demon's hunger — and if the wolf is on the wrong side of the river, why then, the Demon will hunt it there!

Crossing will be easy. The Neck isn't far ahead and the ice will

help its master. Soon the wolf will lie helpless at the Demon's feet:
poisoned, unable to move, its bright souls fluttering in terror...

'Den's not far now,' panted Dark.

Renn didn't reply. She'd spotted another mutilated birch. Naiginn had slashed its trunk to ribbons, but what puzzled her was that he'd done it some time ago: the tree-blood had hardened and turned white.

The wind was rising, the pines roaring on the heights. Amid the tumult she thought she heard demons howling their hunger and hatred to the storm.

Dark paused for breath, the wind whipping his cobwebby hair about his face. 'You hear them too?'

'I've been sensing them since we reached the coast.'

'I think they're drawn to Naiginn.'

'But where is he?' she said. 'These trees... He did this days ago!'

They struggled on through slushy drifts and over streams treacherous with rotten ice. The net was heavy on Renn's shoulder, its weights bumping against her back. She felt helpless without her bow. What use were her axe and her slingshot?

She thought of the egg-shaped sink-stone in her medicine pouch. Should she tie it to the net to increase its power? Or had it been given to her for some other purpose? She didn't *know*.

She hated to think of Torak alone on the other side of the river. Naiginn's marks on that side had been fresh. What if they'd got it wrong and Naiginn was over there now, stalking Torak with a quiver of poisoned arrows?

Rounding the bend, she almost walked into Dark. 'The Den,' he said dully. 'It's gone.'

Downhill through the trees they made out the mountain of shattered ice that was choking the Neck. Behind it, meltwater had turned the valley into a wind-tossed lake clogged with dead trees and the bloated bodies of horses and deer. Somewhere beneath it lay the Den. Renn pictured Darkfur trapped in the cavern she'd dug for her cubs, the black water rushing in...

'Over here!' Dark was beckoning. He'd found paw-prints in the snow.

'They're Wolf's,' said Renn, who knew his tracks as well as she knew Torak's. 'Looks like he found the Den gone, then headed uphill.'

They looked at each other. Renn snapped her fingers. 'Of course, the spare Den! Maybe Darkfur's up there and Wolf's gone to find her!'

'And maybe Naiginn's there too,' warned Dark.

After a long tense climb they reached the granite outcrop where Darkfur had dug her second Den, cleverly concealing the entrance beneath an overhanging boulder. There was no sign of Naiginn, and Wolf was nowhere to be seen – although lots of fresh paw-prints told them he'd been here recently.

Blackear was watching warily from the trees, and Pebble came bounding down and greeted them briefly before resuming his guard on the Den. From deep within came Darkfur's muffled grunt-whines, and a thin high mewing.

'She's had her cubs!' cried Renn.

Dark didn't reply. He was striding about looking for tracks.

The hairs on the back of Renn's neck began to prickle, and at the corner of her eye she glimpsed a thin shadow slip behind a pine. Grasping the amulet at her throat, she muttered a charm to ward off the demon. Moments later, Rip swooped with a stony kek-kek-kek! and chased it into the Forest.

Shortly afterwards, Rek alighted on a rock and greeted Renn with a rattling gurgle. Solemnly she bowed to the raven. 'Stay here, little grandfather,' she told the bird. 'Protect this place from demons.'

'Something's not right,' said Dark. 'I can't find any trace of Naiginn. No tracks, no slashed trees.'

'And all I can sense are lesser demons.'

'So where is he?'

'He was at the main Den, I'm sure of it.'

'What are we missing?'

A puzzling thought occurred to her. 'Fin-Kedinn must have *known* the main Den was flooded, he knows everything that goes on around camp – so why didn't he tell us?'

Dark was nodding. 'It's as if he wanted us out of the way. And he also knows that she-wolves dig spare Dens.'

'But Naiginn doesn't know that. Maybe that's why there's no trace of him—'

'—because he was never here!' Dark looked horrified. 'Oh, Renn, I've got it all wrong!'

'But where *is* he?'

'Down there,' he said in an altered voice.

'Where?

'Look!' He pointed. 'He's near the Neck – on the *other* side of the river! And there's Torak, heading straight for him!'

The little demon fled shrieking through the trees and Wolf went flying after it.

He pursued it all the way to a gully near the top of the ridge. He cornered it, chased it into a crack between the roots of a fierce old pine. *There.* Now it couldn't escape. The tree knew its work, it would hold the demon fast in its roots.

Giving himself a shake, Wolf loped back to the spare Den to rejoin his pack. In the Up the Thunderer's growls were getting louder, its chill breath raking Wolf's fur. Trees were thrashing and roaring. He heard lemmings, badgers, foxes taking shelter in their burrows.

Blackear was patrolling the Forest, Pebble and the ravens keeping watch over the Den. At the entrance Wolf

210

snuffed the wonderful sweet smell of newborn cub. He heard their squeaky mews and the steady rasp of Darkfur licking them clean. He longed to crawl inside and lick them too – but he knew that if he tried, his mate would growl him away. His place was outside, keeping them safe from bears, wolverines and demons.

Leaping onto a rock, Wolf slitted his eyes against the wind. From far below came the noise of the Fast Wet fighting the mountain of Bright Hard Cold. Through the trees he saw the pack-sister and the good pale-pelted tailless making their way laboriously downhill.

Next moment he spotted movement on the other side of the valley. It was Tall Tailless. He too was heading for the Bright Hard Cold, staring at the ground as he sometimes did when he was stalking prey. He hadn't seen the pale-pelted demon, only a few lopes ahead.

Watch out! Wolf howled urgently. *Danger!*

Tall Tailless straightened and cast about. He still hadn't seen the demon. But the demon had heard Wolf's howls, it was staring intently across the Fast Wet.

Wolf didn't know what to do. He had to stay here and protect Darkfur and the cubs from the other demons menacing the Den.

But Tall Tailless needed him too.

TWENTY-SIX

Naiginn was snaking between the trees on his long bone skates, drawing ever closer to the ice mountain. He hadn't seen Torak labouring after him.

Torak's hastily made snowshoes were nightmarishly slow, and the wind was screaming, buffeting him back. Ahead of him the ice mountain was a frozen chaos of jutting floes and tilting slabs, stark white against the purple-black storm clouds that were turning day to dusk. The Forest was thrashing and groaning: at any moment the World Spirit would spear the clouds and unleash the storm. At any moment the furious river might crash through the ice, engulfing both Torak and Naiginn in a torrent they would not survive.

The demon had reached the foot of the ice and kicked off his skates. He stood craning his neck, seeking a way up. His mouth was stretched in an ugly leer that laid bare his hunger for Wolf's souls.

Creeping closer, Torak whipped an arrow from his quiver. The wind was blasting him, he had to brace his legs as he prepared to shoot. Now was his chance to make Renn and his pack-brother safe for ever.

The instant he let fly, a gust nearly knocked him off his feet and his shot went wide, thudding into a trunk a handsbreadth from Naiginn. The demon spun round: *'You!'*

'Didn't think I'd catch you?' shouted Torak above the trees' roar. 'Surely the great Naiginn can't have made a mistake?'

'I never make mistakes,' spat the demon. 'You're *nothing*, I'll crush you like a fly!'

'I won't let you kill Wolf!'

'You can't stop me! Don't you realize the ice is on *my* side?'

'And the Forest's on mine!'

Suddenly the sky went black, as if a gigantic hand had blotted out the sun. An ear-splitting crack of thunder, a dazzle of lightning – then hail was hammering down: bigger than slingstones and sharper than flint, shredding bark, smashing branches and punishing trees, battering Torak with bruising force.

Naiginn threw back his head and howled with glee. 'See? The ice is helping *me*! Your Forest is *weak*, it'll never conquer *ice!'* With preternatural skill he swarmed up the frozen mountain.

Torak tore off his snowshoes and started after him.

The ice had teeth, it was like climbing knives – and it was doing its best to fling him off, snapping handholds and crumbling beneath his feet. As he reached the top he made out Naiginn a few paces ahead, picking his way with inhuman ease around yawning gaps in the ice and the jutting skeletons of trees.

Hail pelted Torak in blinding waves. It tried to trip him, rolling treacherously under his boots. Slabs jolted unsteadily when he trod on them. A rotten floe broke beneath him, plunging him knee-deep in freezing meltwater.

Naiginn had seen him and was taking aim with his bow. Torak dodged, the shot missing his chest and grazing his palm. Reaching behind for his quiver, he found it empty: the arrows must have fallen out as he climbed. He threw the quiver aside and stumbled on, keeping his bow in case he came on a spent arrow. His slingshot would have been better, he could have used hail for missiles, but he seemed to have dropped it too. And Naiginn still had all his weapons: bow, axe, knife, harpoon.

Amid the hail's thunderous onslaught Torak heard thin, evil voices as cold as slivers of ice. *The master's strongest of all!* crowed the lesser demons. *Soon the wolf will be his!*

A red mist descended on Torak, and he flung his axe at Naiginn's departing back. The weapon bounced off a floe and toppled into the swirling floodwaters below. Now all he had was his knife – and a bow without any arrows.

All over now! jeered the demons. *Why don't you follow your axe and jump in too?*

Torak cast about for something else to throw. Icicles hung like daggers: he grabbed one, tried to snap it off. Too hard, too slippery, he couldn't get a grip.

'The ice is on *my* side, remember?' taunted Naiginn.

Torak ran to the remains of a pine and took hold of a branch. His fingers felt strangely clumsy but he managed to snap it off.

As he tried to make the throw, he overbalanced and nearly toppled over the edge of the ice. He swayed. Below him the lake was a dizzying tumult of wind-tossed waves and rocking debris. His feet felt weirdly distant from the rest of him.

Naiginn threw back his head and crowed with laughter. 'Don't you know what's happening, spirit walker? *Wolfbane,* remember? All it takes is a scratch! *The poison's inside you!* There's nothing you can do!'

Torak stared at the beads of blood on his hand. His knees sagged. He was finding it hard to stand.

'Soon you won't be able to feel your feet,' gloated Naiginn. 'Then your legs will go numb, then your whole body! Heart fluttering like a trapped bird, lungs failing, every breath a torment! You'll be weak as water – but still conscious, oh, yes, I want you aware! I want you to watch me eating your wolf alive!'

Is that why he doesn't finish me off? Torak thought hazily. Next moment he saw a sight that jolted him alert like an icy deluge. Directly ahead, on the slope above the Neck, Wolf was flying downhill towards them: towards Naiginn.

Stay back! Torak tried to howl, but his voice was lost in the din of the hail. In horror he saw Wolf nearing the ice mountain – which, on this side of the river, was far less steep. Now Wolf was hurtling towards the demon, his black lips peeled back in a snarl as he raced to defend his pack-brother.

Naiginn had seen him and was reaching for another arrow. Belatedly, Torak realized he still had the branch in his hand. He flung it, striking the demon on the shoulder, making him fall to his knees.

It wouldn't stop him for long, Torak had only moments to get Wolf out of the way.

Pack-brother, to me! he barked – and Wolf, hearing that he was in deadly earnest, swerved on one forepaw and shot past Naiginn, leaping a fallen tree and skittering into Torak with such force he nearly pushed him off the ice.

The demon was moving sideways around the tree to get a clear shot. He was only ten paces away. If Wolf stayed with Torak, Naiginn couldn't miss.

No time for wolf talk. 'I do this to save you!' Torak shouted at his pack-brother.

Then he grabbed Wolf by the scruff and flung him into the lake.

TWENTY-SEVEN

Slitting her eyes against the hail, Renn followed Dark down the slope. He was running in Wolf's tracks: she kicked off her snowshoes and copied him.

The hillside was thick with willows, but through them she made out the storm-tossed floodwaters battering the ice mountain. Amid the debris she spotted Wolf's upturned muzzle: he was swimming towards a fallen pine jutting from the bank.

She saw Naiginn at the top of the ice mountain, trying to take aim. The pine was in the way. With a snarl he started down the ice. He hadn't seen Renn or Dark.

Dark grabbed her shoulder. 'Make sure you stay out of my way!' he shouted above the din of the hail. 'I don't want to shoot you instead of the demon!'

'Yes, but I'll need to get closer, or the net won't catch his souls!'

He thought for a moment, jerked his head at a clump of boulders to his right, where the trees were thinner. 'I'll go that way, you stay this side!'

They separated, Renn losing Wolf's trail and floundering through drifts.

That was when she saw Torak. He stood high on the ice with no weapon but his knife, staring at his pack-brother swimming for the bank. Naiginn was intent on reaching Wolf; if he glanced round and saw Torak he would kill him with a single shot.

Frantically Renn waved at him: *Get down!* she told him silently.

He felt her eyes on him and turned. He was swaying, his face chalk-white, eyes unnaturally wide – but she couldn't see any blood. What was wrong?

Wolfbane, he mouthed.

Net or no net, she had to do something to save him. Yanking her slingshot from her belt, she wrenched open her medicine pouch.

As she fumbled for the stone egg, she was dimly aware of the scrape of a dog sled beyond the rocks where Dark was heading. She couldn't see who it was – but Naiginn could. Hefting his harpoon, he sent it hurtling over the rocks. A crash, yelps of terrified dogs – and the demon hooted in triumph.

Renn found the stone egg. Why didn't Dark shoot? As she loaded her slingshot she saw Wolf scramble onto the pine and shake the water from his fur.

Naiginn spotted Renn and broke into a grin. 'Too late!' he shrieked. 'The wolf is *mine!*'

Torak could no longer feel the onslaught of the storm. Through the pummelling hail he made out Renn and Dark on the bank, Renn loading her slingshot, Dark higher up, backing towards a clump of rocks with a spear, trying to get a clear view of the demon.

Naiginn had reached the foot of the ice and was picking his way towards Wolf, who'd clambered onto a fallen pine and was shaking the wet from his fur. The demon couldn't make the shot: the tree's towering root disc was in the way.

Renn swung her slingshot and struck him in the back. He staggered, nearly fell. '*By power of rock and river,*' she shouted, her red hair flying as she ran towards him down the slope. '*By power of earth and tree – I turn your evil against you!*' Still chanting the curse, she whipped the net from her shoulder and made ready to cast. Dark was waving and yelling at her: 'Renn, get out of the way!'

Suddenly Torak spotted one of his own arrows lying almost within reach. And he still had his bow…

The sky seemed to darken still further as Renn's voice

rose above the clamour of the storm: *'With this net I bind you! With this curse I banish you!'*

For a moment Naiginn faltered, and it seemed to Torak that Renn's words were thin black roots whipping around the demon's limbs, binding him fast and dragging him back.

Clumsily Torak groped for the arrow. Below him Naiginn was swaying, intent on Wolf. Setting his teeth, Torak fitted the arrow to the string. He took aim. Naiginn was directly below him: even weakened by poison, Torak *knew* he could make this shot...

'To the Otherworld I send you!' intoned Renn. *'Never to return – not till fire freezes and stone burns – not till Sea is dust and Time is dead!'*

Torak let fly. But at the same instant Wolf made a great soaring leap at Naiginn, and Torak's arrow struck him full in the flank.

'No!' gasped Torak.

'He's *mine!*' screamed Naiginn. Whipping out his knife, he lunged at Wolf's motionless body lying half-in and half-out of the water – but something jerked him back: his parka had snagged on a branch. Snarling, he twisted round to free himself. Couldn't do it, the Forest refused to let him go.

Torak fell to his knees. His legs wouldn't obey him. He heaved himself forwards on his elbows in a frantic bid to reach Wolf. He was too high up, he wouldn't make it. In horror he watched Naiginn rip free and stand astride Wolf, raising his knife.

Dimly, Torak was aware of Dark still yelling at Renn, who was pushing through the willows towards Naiginn. As Dark took aim with his spear, a man staggered from behind the boulders and wrenched it from his grip. Fin-Kedinn's face was ashen, his mouth set in a hard line, one hand clutching a dark stain on his side. Drawing back his arm, he threw the spear with all his might. It sped towards Naiginn, skewering him in the belly with such force that it flung him off his feet and pinned him to the ice.

Now Torak felt a groaning shudder beneath him. The river's pent-up rage could no longer be withstood: the ice mountain was about to give way.

With a last desperate effort Torak half-slid, half-tumbled towards the bank, where Dark was lifting Wolf's limp body and slinging it over his shoulder.

'We've got to get higher!' shouted Dark. Hooking his free arm around Torak, he hauled him to his feet and staggered uphill. 'Renn, go *higher*! It's going to collapse!'

'I've beaten you, spirit walker!' cackled Naiginn behind them.

Over his shoulder Torak saw the demon baring his bloody teeth and clutching the spear-shaft jutting from his belly. 'The wolf is dead... I've *won*!'

Then Renn's net was flying through the air and engulfing him where he lay – and the power of the Widewater and the Blackwater, the greatest rivers in the Open Forest and the Deep, was bursting through the ice and spewing the demon out to Sea.

But higher up the slope, as Torak felt the poison draining the last of his strength, he only had eyes for Wolf. Dark had placed him under a rowan tree and he lay on his side, Torak's arrow jutting from his flank. His tongue lolled. His eyes were shut. He wasn't moving.

'No!' gasped Torak. 'No, no, no, no, *no!*'

TWENTY-EIGHT

Torak is drowning in a sea of poison. He can't see, can't hear. Can't feel his limbs or shout for help.

Dimly he became aware of the thunder of the river and the crunch of debris rushing past. Somewhere a girl was crying as if her heart would break.

Slowly, with enormous effort, he opened his eyes.

He was lying on his side beneath the rowan tree, nose to nose with Wolf. Behind him and not far off he could hear Renn sobbing, and Dark murmuring words he couldn't make out. It came to him that they thought he was dead.

The wind had dropped and the hail had turned to snow, big fluffy flakes settling softly on Wolf's fur. Too weak for wolf talk or human speech, Torak spoke to his pack-brother in his mind: *You can't leave me.*

Wolf's eyelids flickered, and his amber gaze met Torak's – but only for a heartbeat. The glow faded, the eyelids lowered... and Wolf breathed his last breath.

No! cried Torak in his head. But what lay beside him was an empty husk. Wolf's spirit was gone.

Torak's desperation hardened to flinty resolve. *I will not let you die!*

There was only one thing to do and the danger would be enormous: never before had Torak spirit walked in a dying creature. With no black root to help him, he might be unable to do it; or Wolf's souls might already be beyond reach; or Torak's poisoned heart might give out before his own souls could return to his body – but he had to try. He had to see through Wolf's eyes, and perceive what only Wolf could: he had to find Wolf's souls and bring them back.

Maybe because his own souls were already loosened by poison – or because this was Wolf – he felt no stabbing pain or sickening jolt as his souls lifted free of his body. Spirit walking in Wolf was unlike anything he'd ever known. It felt as if he was rediscovering a hidden part of himself that had always been there. It felt like coming home.

Wolf's body was still warm, and Torak found that with an effort he could open his muzzle and draw breath. For a moment he lay feeling the fluffy flakes of Bright Soft Cold settling on his fur, and the ache in his flank where his clumsy pack-brother had shot him by mistake.

Then perception came back in a rush, and suddenly he was perceiving with Wolf's senses. The countless smells and sounds of the Forest were flashing and flickering like sun-dazzle: he heard the Fast Wet sweeping past, and shards of Bright Hard Cold grinding fallen trees; the rowan whispering overhead, a badger digging for worms on the ridge, a family of beavers gnawing bark in the next valley. Much nearer, he caught the pack-sister's sobbing and the salty smell of her tears, the harsh sound of the pale-pelted tailless's wrenching grief – and his pack-brother's beloved Foresty smell. Up at the Den he heard Darkfur suckling her newborn cubs, and Pebble anxiously pacing. He felt a fierce longing to be with his pack, and the bite of worry: who would protect them from demons when he was gone?

This torrent of perception was impossible for Torak to take in, and yet with Wolf's keen awareness he knew at once what mattered and what did not. And what mattered most was finding Wolf's spirit and bringing it back.

Blinking Wolf's eyes, Torak flexed his great paws. He stretched his long sturdy forelegs and his powerful hind legs. He raised his head and lurched to his feet. For an instant Torak's spirit soared with the pure delight of being a wolf. He could swivel his ears and raise his hackles, he had whiskers – and a *tail*!

Then, through the trees, he saw a pulsing, Wolf-shaped glow. The brightest souls in the Forest were walking uphill towards the Den to say goodbye. After that they would climb on to the top of the ridge – and they would keep climbing steadily into the Up, higher and higher until they reached the Tree of Light.

Torak tried to run after Wolf's spirit, but he'd forgotten the arrow in his flank. His forepaws stumbled, his hind legs gave way. Raising his muzzle, he gave a wobbly yowl. *Come – back!*

Wolf's spirit turned its head and met Torak's gaze. Its eyes were alight with love and longing – and resignation. *I can't*, it said.

You must! Again Torak tried to howl, but his strength failed and he slumped to the ground.

Spirit to spirit, he sent one final desperate plea: *You told me you never leave!*

You told me you never leave! Tall Tailless's plea lingered in Wolf's ears.

Far above him in the Up, the Tree of Light was hidden from sight – but he could hear its murmurous rustle and feel its pull: as deep as the pull of mate and cub and pack, though much stronger, and impossible to ignore.

Now Wolf caught the whirr of wings. The three ravens, the black and the white, were circling overhead, cawing encouragement: *Follow!* They would help him reach the Tree of Light.

But he could still hear Tall Tailless. *You told me you never leave!*

As Wolf hesitated among the trees, he spotted the Breath-that-Walks of a tailless walking up the slope. It paused, as if uncertain where to go, and Wolf saw that its forehead and forepaws were marked with the earthy rings which taillesses daub on those who are Not-Breath.

Quork! Quork! The ravens swooped over the tailless, urging it to follow.

Wolf knew that he too must follow the ravens – but it was hard. He could still hear Tall Tailless's plea, and it was making him see flashes from the past. A half-grown Tall Tailless rescuing Wolf from the flooded Den when he was a cub... A full-grown Tall Tailless yip-and-yowling with laughter as Wolf pounces on him from behind... Tall Tailless's narrow silver glance grazing his as they hunt together in the Forest, and in the Mountains, and on the treeless fells at the Edge of the World...

Again Wolf raised his head to the ravens circling in the Up. He thought of the Tree of Light. Then he shook himself, and turned, and trotted back down the slope.

When he reached the rowan tree, he nosed the sodden heap of fur which had been Wolf. He sniffed its rough pads and its whiskery muzzle. Its eyes were half-closed and dull, but in them Wolf caught a spark that was not-wolf. It was the Breath-that-Walks of Tall Tailless.

You have to stay with us, it told him. *Your pack needs you. I need you.*

Wolf swung his tail. *You are very stubborn*, he said.

Torak woke with a jolt.

He was still lying beside Wolf, his hand resting on his pack-brother's flank, which was gently moving.

Wolf's tail twitched. He opened his eyes.

A tear slid down Torak's cheek. *You came back.*

Wolf's cold nose nudged his. *I never leave you.*

Weak with relief, Torak shut his eyes. He felt dizzy, as he always did after spirit walking, but gradually he became aware that his body was no longer numb. He could *feel* the chill of the earth beneath him, and his pack-brother's coarse fur under his fingers. In some way that he didn't understand, spirit walking in Wolf had cleansed his body of the poison: like fire searing a wound.

Behind him, Renn was still crying as if her heart would break, and Dark was speaking to her quietly, his voice cracking with grief. Torak wanted to reassure them, tell them he wasn't dead – but he couldn't summon the strength.

Then in an icy rush he realized that they weren't crying for him.

'No, Fin-Kedinn, no!' sobbed Renn. 'You can't die!'

'Renn, come away,' Dark said brokenly. 'It's over. He's gone.'

TWENTY-NINE

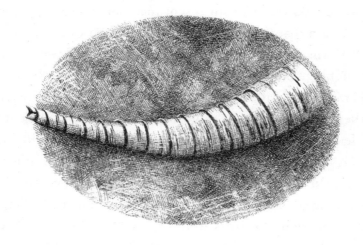

'**S**hamik brought food,' said Torak.

'I'm not hungry,' Renn said without turning her head.

'It's been a day and a night. You need to eat.'

'No.'

They were talking in undertones to avoid angering the dead man's souls: Torak's voice gentle, Renn's rough with grief.

The hail had left red welts on her hands and neck, but those on her face were hidden by mourning marks: grim grey bands of river clay smeared across her brow and down her cheeks. She looked stony and remote. A Mage, not a mate.

The flood had subsided and below them the Elk River glided swift and strong. Fin-Kedinn lay where he'd died. Renn knelt beside him, combing his hair.

Yesterday she'd allowed the distraught Ravens to place him on a litter; then she'd sent them away, breaking the tradition that the dead man must be taken to the Death Platform on the day of death. Alarmed, the Ravens had sought guidance from the new Leader they'd chosen. Dark had told them that as the fallen one had never seen their new camp on the ridge, his spirit couldn't trouble it. He'd given Renn three days to prepare the body.

A flock of geese flew honking overhead and Torak watched them pass. Spring had burst on the Forest with startling suddenness, and the valley echoed with trickling and gurgling; the trees were alive with birdsong. It felt cruel. How could it be spring without Fin-Kedinn?

Renn asked what he was making, and he showed her the stick of stripped yewwood in which he was cutting notches. 'A spirit ladder, to help him find the First—'

'That's for me to do, not you!' she snapped.

'Renn. He was my foster father.'

Tightening her lips, she resumed her work.

The Ravens had taken Fin-Kedinn's bloodstained clothes to be burnt, and she had purified the body with snow and juniper boughs, using special care over the wound in his side. Then she'd dressed him in the new parka and leggings of white reindeer hide which the clan had brought. No boots. The dead must not be able to follow the living.

This isn't happening, thought Torak. How can he be dead? From Kujai and Dark he'd pieced together his foster father's last moments. Fin-Kedinn had taken Kujai's sled and made for the Neck alone, where Naiginn had spotted him and cast his harpoon. Mortally wounded, Fin-Kedinn had staggered from behind the rocks and seized the spear from Dark. Somehow he'd summoned the strength to make that incredible shot before he'd collapsed. Soon afterwards, Kujai had run up and dragged him clear of the flood. He had died in Renn's arms.

Dark had given her earthblood for the Death Marks: purple, as befitted a Leader. Torak stared at the livid rings on the waxen forehead, heart and heels. He had done the same for Fa when he was dying. He remembered how it had felt.

The river had spat Naiginn's body onto rocks near the coast. Both corpse and souls were still entangled in the net, and Dark had lost no time in burning the whole with the last of Renn's bloodstone. Then he'd sewn the ashes into a seal hide which he and the Ravens had tied between granite slabs and taken out to Sea. Dark had dropped it overboard and asked the Sea Mother to ensure that the demon never troubled the living again. As they were making for home, a whale had risen from the waves, and splashed down: the Sea Mother had heard his plea.

Torak shook earthblood from his medicine horn and rubbed it on the spirit ladder. His thoughts circled endlessly. 'I should have been the one to kill the demon,' he'd told Dark earlier. 'I had my chances and I missed. If I hadn't, Fin— my foster father would still be alive.'

'He'd be alive if I hadn't let him grab the spear,' Dark had replied. 'Or if Kujai hadn't let him take the dog sled. If, if, if.'

Of all of them, Renn had been harshest on herself. In the first rawness of her grief she'd screamed at the sky: she should have snatched Fin-Kedinn's bow when she had the chance, she should have seized the spear from Dark...

Torak handed her the spirit ladder and she blinked at it, then laid it beside the body. 'How's your hand?' she asked.

'Dark put on a honey bandage to draw out the last of the wolfbane.'

'Did it work?'

'Feels like it.'

'How's Wolf?'

'Healing fast.' Now was not the time to tell her what he'd seen when he'd spirit walked in his pack-brother. She wasn't listening. She was gazing at the ridge, where black smoke was spiralling into the white sky.

The Ravens were burning the dead man's clothes, weapons, gear. Torak thought of the day five summers ago when he'd watched Fin-Kedinn make a new knife. The Raven Leader had fashioned it with the skill and attention he'd brought to everything he did. Torak hated to think of all that knowledge and care going up in flames.

From the ridge a horn boomed, the echoes winding deep into the hills. Drums answered. Word of the death was spreading.

Fin-Kedinn's own horn would have been put to the fire; what Torak was hearing must be the new horn which Dark had made last night. As Torak had watched his friend winding the cone out of birch-bark strips glued with pine tar, he'd felt a flash of pity. To take over from *Fin-Kedinn*... Men twice Dark's age would have found that a burden too heavy to bear.

Thull came up behind Dark as he sat carving by the fire, making him jump.

'The Salmon Clan wants permission to come to the Death Platform,' said the older man, his scowl making it clear that he disapproved. By custom only the dead man's clan accompanied him on his final journey.

'Tell them they can,' said Dark.

Thull raised his eyebrows. 'Are you sure?'

He nodded. 'After the Thunderstar struck, he led *all* the clans. It's right that anyone who wishes should be allowed to come. Send word to the other clans, will you?'

Thull opened his mouth to protest – then saw that Dark's decision was made, and strode off to do his bidding.

Dark went back to carving lines of power on the rowan logs which would become the Death Platform. In the morning the Ravens would head upriver to a secluded bay on the Widewater and build it.

He knew he'd made the right decision, but he was dreading tomorrow. Particularly the moment when he would have to sing the Death Chant. What if he broke down in front of everyone?

Around him the Ravens were quietly getting ready: preparing food, cleaning clothes, covering weapons so that they couldn't hurt the dead man's souls. Suddenly Dark saw himself as they must see him: a frightened boy struggling to fill a great man's boots. How could he *possibly* lead them?

Grimly he set about staining the marks he'd carved with red, yellow and purple earthblood to protect the body from demons. You'll grow into it, he assured himself. Fin-Kedinn did.

His eyes felt scratchy with fatigue: last night he'd been up and down the valley banishing lesser demons. And always that nagging voice in his head: Maybe you will grow into it, but you'll be alone all your life. Just as Fin-Kedinn was alone…

A shadow fell across him and he raised his head. His belly dropped. It was Kujai.

Dark hadn't seen his friend since he'd left to take the news to his clan. Their goodbyes had been awkward, the Sea-eagle boy unsure how to act now that Dark was Raven Leader as well as Mage. Covertly, Dark watched him hunker down on the other side of the fire and pour wood shavings from palm to palm.

'They found my canoe,' said Kujai. 'It rode the floodwaters. A Salmon Clan hunter brought it back.'

'That's good,' said Dark.

Kujai frowned. 'Thull says you're letting anyone come tomorrow. Can I?'

'Of course.' Dark was dismayed that Kujai felt he needed to ask. So this is what leadership means, he thought unhappily. People don't want to get too close.

'Dark,' Kujai said in a low voice.

'Mm?'

'In a few days my clan's moving camp again.'

'Where to?'

'The Horseleap.'

Dark's spirits plunged. Two valleys to the south. It might as well be ten.

'I used to wonder,' said Kujai without raising his eyes, 'why you don't have a mate. Now I think I know.'

'Why?' Dark said miserably.

Kujai let fall the wood shavings and brushed off his hands. 'Because you've been waiting for me.'

Dark's heart gave a painful jolt.

Raising his head, Kujai gave him a long steady look. 'Have you noticed that the end of your name is the beginning of mine? *Dark – Kujai*. They go together. That means something, I think.'

Of course Dark had noticed. He was overjoyed that Kujai had too.

'Dark,' said Kujai with a hint of a smile. 'If you want me to stay, you have to tell me!'

'I want you to stay,' he blurted out. 'With me, with the

Ravens, for ever.' He tried to smile but his heart was too full. Kujai came round to his side of the fire and knelt and took Dark's hands in his. 'Then I will,' he said.

This isn't happening, Renn thought numbly. How can we be having a procession without Fin-Kedinn?

They'd started at dawn on the long walk upstream, and now the sun was high in a sky of merciless blue. Buds were bursting, catkins trembling, chaffinches and woodlarks singing in the trees. The first spring after the Thunderstar, and the Forest was healing. Why wasn't Fin-Kedinn here to see it?

Dark was leading the way. Then came the men bearing the body, then Renn and Torak and the rest of the Ravens, followed by the Sea-eagles and the Salmon Clan. Fin-Kedinn's old dog Grip had soon lagged behind; Kujai was carrying him in his arms.

Torak looked gaunt, the scar on his cheek stark in the sunlight. Renn knew that at night he went with the wolves and howled his grief to the moon. She wanted to do that too, but she felt as if she'd been turned to stone.

Was Fin-Kedinn's spirit here now, watching from the Forest? Why couldn't she feel him? *Had* she done the Death Marks right? Had she kept his souls together?

Torak touched her shoulder. 'Look behind you,' he murmured.

She glanced over her shoulder – and gasped. On the bank, the Sea-eagles had been joined by the Whale and Viper Clans. Amid the dazzle on the river she saw many canoes paddling after them: Kelp Clan, Cormorant, Seal. High on the ridge, Willow Clan hunters were raising their bows in salute as they started downhill. Up ahead stood the Otter Clan, waiting with the Red Deer Clan and the Bats. All had come to honour the man who'd brought them together after the Thunderstar, and given them hope when they needed it most.

At last they passed the place where the two rivers flowed together, and soon afterwards they halted and built the Death Platform. Dark had chosen a grove of watchful hollies overlooking the Widewater, the river Fin-Kedinn had done so much to save. They laid him facing the Mountains – so that, like the salmon, his spirit could make its final journey upstream.

Renn covered the body with a cloth of finest wovenbark, a gift from the Red Deer. No warmth in it, she thought desolately. And he'll be cold without his boots.

She remembered the white elk they had seen together on the day she and Torak had left to find Wolf. Had Fin-Kedinn known that it had come for him?

Torak put his hands on her shoulders and drew her gently away from the body. 'Don't let your shadow fall on it, you'll get sick.'

Rip, Rek and Ark came to perch in a holly near the Death Platform. Renn bowed to them. 'Do your work,' she urged the guardians in a low voice. 'Help him find the First Tree.'

In the grove people were sharing food: dried salmon cakes, reed-pollen bread, auroch-gut sausages, seal liver. While they ate they told memories of the dead man, taking care not to mention him by name, for fear of attracting his spirit. Renn found that she had nothing to say. All she could recall was that terrible moment when he'd fallen to his knees, clutching his side.

When the food was finished, Dark rose to his feet. He was even paler than usual, nerving himself to sing the Death Chant.

Suddenly an old man shambled out of the Forest and quietly asked Dark if he could sing it instead. The Walker was almost unrecognizable. Mourning marks lent his face a ravaged dignity, and he'd tamed his mane and beard; even his rags were clean (for him). At a nod from Dark, he drew himself up, and in a rich, deep voice he sang his old friend to peace.

After the song was over, Dark put his fists to his chest and bowed to the body. 'May your guardian fly with you,' he said simply. 'May you reach the First Tree – and find peace!' His voice cracked. Kujai came forwards and put an arm around his shoulders. Together they walked away.

People were beginning to leave. In life Fin-Kedinn had eaten the creatures of the Forest, and now in death they would feed on him. Three moons later, Renn would retrieve his bones and place them in the Raven bone-ground. She was already dreading that.

'It was well done,' said Durrain, Leader and Mage of the Red Deer Clan.

'He has gone beyond the clouds,' agreed Watash.

But *has* he? wondered Renn.

What tormented her was that she had no memory of putting on the Death Marks. She remembered Dark giving her the earthblood and making sure that she used the finger protected by her finger-guard – but after that, nothing.

So how would she ever know if she'd done it right?

Dusk was falling and Torak and Renn were alone in the glade. People had been careful to cover their tracks as they left, so that the spirit couldn't follow them home, and there had been no crying and no looking back.

Wolf appeared among the trees. Grip, lying beneath the Death Platform, uttered a low growl. Wolf avoided the old dog and skirted the other side of the glade to reach Torak.

At last Renn tore herself away from the Death Platform. Torak noticed that she wasn't covering her tracks, so he did it for her. 'Don't!' she snapped.

'But the souls might follow—'

'Then let them!'

'Renn.'

She turned on him. 'How can you bear to push him away? How can you *bear* it?'

'I can't. But—'

'You brought Wolf back from the dead!' she cried accusingly. 'Why couldn't you bring him back too?' Flinging herself at him, she pummelled his chest with her fists. '*Why?*' she sobbed. Then he was holding her in his arms and she was crying great wrenching sobs. Wolf came and leant against them with his ears down and his tail between his legs.

Some time later, as they were walking downriver, Renn said bitterly, 'The Kelps are right to keep something of their dead. I wish we could too.'

'We have,' said Torak. 'He swapped wrist-guards with you, remember? And he swapped knives with Dark. And the day before he died, he gave Thull his amulet to give to me.' He showed her the little yewwood raven which Dark had carved for Fin-Kedinn last summer. 'He knew we'd want something of his when he was gone, and he made sure that we got it.'

Renn fingered the wrist-guard of polished antler which her uncle had incised with swooping ravens and running deer.

'He knew what he was doing, Renn,' Torak went on. 'He wanted to stop us killing the demon and being cast out, and he wanted to prevent Dark becoming a killer. He wanted to end his own pain too. He found a way to do all that. And I think – I think even if I'd known he was dying and I'd tried to bring him back, he wouldn't have come.'

She sniffed. 'But the Death Marks,' she said wearily.

'What about them?'

'I can't remember putting them on! I don't know if I did it right!'

'Of course you did.'

'But you can't be sure!'

'Yes, Renn, I can.' At last he told her what he'd seen when he was spirit walking in Wolf. 'His souls were together, I saw them. And Renn – he wasn't limping, he was *walking*! No more pain.'

Again she sniffed, and wiped her nose on her wrist. 'No more pain,' she mumbled.

Torak put his arm around her. 'Come on, it's getting dark.'

It was past middle-night when they reached their camp. Darkfur was underground with the cubs, who wouldn't leave the Den for another moon. Pebble and Blackear gave them a subdued welcome.

Moths flitted among the trees. A hare rose on its hind legs and bounded away. 'The First Tree is so bright,' said Renn, gazing at the sky. 'I think the guardians have done their work. I think he's at peace.'

For a long time they stood together, watching the luminous green ripples in the sky.

And always afterwards, on dark winter nights when the First Tree was shining particularly bright, the clans said it was Fin-Kedinn, stirring the branches and lighting the way for the hunters to come home.

THIRTY

Renn woke to the shrill cries of young swifts swooping after midges. She lay watching the dappled green shade in the shelter, listening to the sounds of happy wolves playing outside: yelps and grunt-whines, the thud of scampering paws.

It was early in the Cloudberry Moon and hot, no need for a sleeping-sack. They were camped near a small lake on the south side of Elk valley, where Darkfur had moved the cubs for the summer. The Raven Clan was in the next valley on the Windriver, near their bone-ground, where yesterday Renn had laid Fin-Kedinn's bones to rest.

Afterwards she had felt so spent that she couldn't even remember hanging up her bow; Torak must have done it for her. He was gone, but he'd left her his food pouch. She munched a salmon cake while oiling her bow, then crawled outside and picked her way around the dried scat and raven pellets to the lake.

Wolf had been keeping cool in the mud, and he rubbed against her, leaving greenish smears. The other wolves bounded to greet her in turn. Then she slipped off her buckskins and waded in, taking care not to wash off her mourning marks.

Rip and Rek were splashing in the shallows, while their three chicks hopped about clamouring for food. Renn was still getting used to the idea of the ravens as a mated pair. She'd always assumed they were brother and sister, and it had come as a shock when they'd taken to holding each other's beaks, then built a large untidy nest in a pine and lined it with underfur plucked from moulting wolves. Their young were fast learners. Already as big as their parents, they could fly, and were adept at teasing wolf cubs.

At nearly four moons old, the cubs were roughly the same age as Wolf had been when Torak had first found him. They were stalking Blackear, who was bounding about with a deer's shinbone in her mouth. Feather, the wiliest cub, was lying in wait behind a juniper bush. Yip, the stockiest, was leaping at Blackear's rump, while Whitepaw was racing ahead to cut her off. Darkfur was sprawled asleep in the shade of her favourite rock. No sign of Pebble: Renn guessed he'd gone looking for Puff, who was the naughtiest cub, always sneaking away to explore.

Renn found Dark and Kujai eating their daymeal among the poplars above the lake. They'd brought Yamna to see the wolves, although as they weren't part of the pack they were keeping a respectful distance.

Yesterday at the bone-grounds Dark had led the rites, and afterwards he'd looked as drained as Renn had felt. He seemed better today, sharing a skin of birch sap with Kujai and working his way through a basket of dried herring roe on kelp.

He offered Renn some, and she took a strip. 'Did you dream of him last night?' he asked.

She nodded. 'But I always see him as he was the day he died. I wish I could remember him as he was before.'

'It'll come,' said Dark.

She nibbled the kelp. 'Have you seen Torak?'

'He's cutting lime bark higher up,' said Kujai, offering the basket to Yamna. The Kelp girl didn't notice: she only had eyes for the wolves. Halut had brought her to be fostered with the Ravens the previous moon and she'd taken to the Forest as if she was born to it; she followed Dark and Kujai around like a puppy, especially if they were going near the pack.

Renn was about to leave when the bracken stirred and Puff emerged, a fluffy bundle of black fur with two bright, inquisitive green eyes. Dark and Kujai pretended not to notice her, but Yamna's jaw dropped. This was the closest she'd ever been to a wolf cub.

'Stay still and let her smell you,' Renn told her quietly. 'No staring, no sudden moves.'

Yamna watched entranced as Puff padded towards her and sniffed her bare toes.

'Talk to her softly,' said Dark. 'It'll reassure her.'

'And if you smile,' said Renn, 'try not to bare your teeth. I did once when Wolf was young, he got really confused.'

'I am so honoured,' Yamna told the cub solemnly. 'You are the most beautiful wolf I've ever seen.'

Mewing and lashing her tail, Puff put her forepaws on Yamna's knee and grabbed the neck of her jerkin in her needle-sharp teeth.

Renn chuckled. 'I forgot to warn you, they chew *everything*! There's a reason I've tied back my hair.'

It wasn't long before Darkfur arrived with Pebble and shooed the errant cub back to the others. Dark stood up and said they must be heading back to camp; he pre-empted Yamna's protests by telling her they could pick cloudberries on the way. Renn headed off to find Torak.

It was already late afternoon: she must have slept most of the day. The undergrowth was lush with ferns, blue cranesbill and yellow suncups. Through the trees she glimpsed a roe buck nibbling willows. It sensed that she wasn't hunting and went on eating.

The closeness between Dark and Kujai had made Renn impatient to be with Torak. She thought of his smooth brown shoulders and the veins on his arms; the green flecks in his narrow grey eyes.

'*Cloudberries!*' Yamna's voice floated on the breeze.

Renn stopped in her tracks. A memory had just come to her. She was ten summers old, picking cloudberries with Fin-Kedinn. They had filled a birch-bark pail and he was pouring a stream of honey-sweet berries into her mouth. She was standing with her head back, gaping like a baby bird – and for a joke he'd kept on pouring, even when her mouth was overflowing and she was fumbling to catch them in her hands. Soon they were laughing so hard they could barely stand...

Renn found herself smiling and blinking back tears.

At the next stream she came to, she knelt and looked at her name-soul's broken image in the water. Then she splashed her face and started washing off her mourning marks.

The pack-sister was busy washing her muzzle, so Wolf gave her arm a brief jaw-hold by way of greeting, and continued on his way.

He and Darkfur followed the scent of newborn fawn to a blackthorn thicket, where they found it lurching to its feet, bawling while its mother licked it clean. Wolf darted in to grab it, but the mother lashed out with her head-branches; she was so determined that they soon gave up.

Later when they returned, the doe and her fawn had gone, leaving behind her delicious slippery afterbirth. Wolf let Darkfur eat it all, then she headed back to sick it up for the cubs, while he went to find Tall Tailless.

As he ran, Wolf revelled in the feel of cool earth beneath his pads and the rich smells flowing over his nose. He was *happy*. The Forest was full of prey, and all the cubs were still alive. And Tall Tailless and the pack-sister weren't feeling so sad.

Wolf found his pack-brother putting tree hide in a little Fast Wet. They touched noses and Tall Tailless gave Wolf a deeply satisfying scratch in the itchy spot between his shoulders that he could never reach himself. Then they howled to warn stranger wolves to stay out of their range. Then they just sat.

Can you hear the Tree of Light? said Tall Tailless. *Even now, when you can't see it?*

Wolf was surprised. *Of course I can. It's still there in the Up.*

His pack-brother was silent. He had changed since he'd shot Wolf by mistake. He was better at understanding what Wolf meant, and in some way Wolf didn't understand, he seemed to be both not-wolf and real wolf at the same time. Although, Wolf thought fondly, his poor little nose remained as useless as ever.

Do you remember what happened after I shot you? Tall Tailless asked suddenly.

Wolf glanced at him, then away. *I was leaving. Then I heard you howl.*

247

Tall Tailless plucked a tuft of underfur from Wolf's flank and let it drift on the breeze. *I'm glad you came back,* he said.

Wolf stood up, swinging his tail. He rubbed his forehead under his pack-brother's jaw. *Me too,* he replied.

Wolf had returned to Darkfur and the cubs, and Torak was putting his last bundle of lime bark to soak in the stream.

He remembered Fa teaching him rope-making when he was little. A few summers later, when he'd just learnt that he was a spirit walker and was feeling frightened and confused, he had watched Fin-Kedinn putting bundles of bark to soak; he'd felt steadied simply by being with him.

It still hurt to think of his foster father – it always would – but after three moons the pain wasn't quite so fierce.

You're feeling better, Wolf had said before he left. He didn't only mean about Fin-Kedinn, he meant Torak's souls. And he was right.

Torak didn't understand what had happened, but for a heartbeat, after he'd spirit walked in Wolf and before he'd returned to his own body, their souls had flowed together. In that instant Torak had felt a great brightness cleansing his damaged spirit. Since then it was as if only the good had remained: the exhilaration of flying, the wild joy of being a Sea wolf, the deep connectedness of trees.

He understood now why the Kelps made no attempt to keep things of the Forest separate from those of the Sea. To them it was all one: the Forest under the Sea, the Forest on land, and the Forest in the sky. It occurred to Torak that if this was true, then by spirit walking in trees he might one day be able to venture under the Sea, and even up to the First Tree. It was a dizzying thought, both perilous and alluring...

'There you are!' cried Renn, making her way through the undergrowth.

Like him she was barefoot and wore a sleeveless jerkin and calf-length leggings. Her pale skin was dappled with leafy sunlight, and against the green bracken her red hair flamed.

But something about her was different. It took him a moment to realize what. 'You've washed off your mourning marks!'

She broke into a grin. 'It felt like the right time.'

Coming close, she ran her hands up his arms, raising little shivers of heat. They kissed. When they drew apart, he took her face in his hands and studied her. 'The Kelps are right,' he said. 'You do have a horribly round head.'

She laughed and punched him in the chest. 'And your blunt little teeth, so un-wolf-like!'

He fetched the trout he'd caught earlier, which had been keeping fresh in the stream, and they started back to camp.

Renn told him about Yamna's encounter with Puff. 'You should have seen her face! I think she's plotting to stay with the Ravens for ever.'

By the time they reached camp the sky was a deep twilit blue, and bats were flickering over the lake.

Rip and Rek were roosting together, and their chicks were huddled in an adjacent pine with their heads under their wings. The wolves were stretching and lashing their tails, encouraging each other for the hunt. The cubs were racing about, yipping excitedly: they were going with their elders under Pebble's watchful eye.

Watching them reminded Torak how it had felt to be Wolf: perceiving everything in the Forest with such intensity, such ease...

Renn turned her head and gave him a narrow look. 'You are not going to become a wolf,' she said drily. 'I won't let you.'

He laughed. 'I wasn't thinking of—'

'Yes, you were.'

'Not of becoming one – of *being* one. It felt so right.'

'Well, this is right too.'

He linked his fingers in hers. 'Yes. It is.'

While she cleaned and gutted the trout, he woke a fire, then they set the fish to roast. Wolf began to howl and the other wolves joined in, including the cubs with their wobbly yowls. Torak howled with them. Then he stood watching Renn watching the fire.

The wind had dropped and the Forest was hushed. In

the distance the sound of the rapids at the Neck was like the beat of a great heart.

Torak thought of the Burnt Lands to the east, which had been blasted by the Thunderstar but were now hazed with green, drifts of dark-pink willowherb healing the charred valleys. He watched the pack disappearing among the trees.

Wolf felt Torak's eyes on him and looked back. He swung his tail and they exchanged a brief warm glance. Then Wolf turned and trotted into the Forest.

Wolfbane is the ninth and final book in the classic series that began with *Wolf Brother*.

AUTHOR'S NOTE

The world of Torak and Renn is that of six thousand years ago. That's after the Ice Age, but before farming spread to northern Scandinavia – when the land was one vast Forest.

The people looked like you or me, but they were hunter-gatherers. They lived in small clans, some staying at a campsite for a few days or moons, others staying put all year round. They didn't have writing, metals or the wheel – but they didn't need them. They were superb survivors. They knew all about the animals, trees, plants and rocks on which they survived. When they wanted something they knew where to find it, or how to make it.

Like the other books in the series, *Wolfbane* takes place in northern Scandinavia, so the wildlife is appropriate to the region – as are the seasonal changes in the hours of daylight. However I've changed mountains, rivers and coastlines to suit the stories, which means that you won't find the specific features of Torak's world in a modern atlas.

Kelp Island is based on my 2016 research trip to Haida Gwaii in British Columbia and to Alaska. Like Renn, I almost got stuck on a very sticky green mudflat. And I too struggled through an incredibly tangled rainforest: it took me two hours to cover less than two miles, by which time I was covered in mud and spruce needles. While bushwhacking in the forest, my guide told me how she'd once retrieved a salmon dropped by an eagle being mobbed by ravens. She said she'd eaten the fish for her supper. That's why Wolf gets his salmon in *Wolfbane*. Also on Haida Gwaii, I was able to get close to several huge eagles' nests, and the young captain of our little ship told me how once he'd camped in such a nest overnight. That's why Torak and Renn camp in one too.

The ghostly remains of the Ancestors' village was inspired by two locations separated by thousands of miles. First, a moss-smothered, half-made dugout we found in the rainforest on Haida Gwaii; sadly it had been abandoned by ancestral Haida people who had fallen victim to smallpox. Secondly and nearer to home, by the Scowles in Paynes' Wood, Gloucestershire, which Jonathan Wright kindly showed me after we'd been down his Clearwell Caves in the Royal Forest of Dean.

Much of the icy detail in the story comes from my January 2020 trip down the Norwegian coast on the Hurtigruten Line. And Torak and Renn's coastal foraging is based on that of the First Nations of the Pacific Northwest. I too have munched delicious slices of giant scallop taken fresh from a rock pool, and dried herring roe on kelp fronds, prepared in the traditional Haida way. While beach-combing in Alaska and Haida Gwaii, I've grazed on kelp, dulse, ulva, sugar kelp and sea asparagus. And in common with Dark and Kujai I've snacked on toasted sea wrack. Also known as 'Indian popcorn', it's deliciously crunchy, and really does taste like popcorn. I should add that herring shoals really were once so closely packed that one could literally rake in the fish, as the clans do in *Wolfbane*. Their herring rakes are based on a traditional Nootka design.

Torak's underwater spirit walking was inspired by my experience of snorkelling with wild killer whales off Tysfjord, north Norway in 2005, as well as snorkelling in Alaska in 2016 – another exhilarating experience, which was enlivened by the presence of a humpback whale feeding a few yards away.

Concerning wolves, I was a patron of the UK Wolf Conservation Trust from 2004 until the Trust closed to the public and the wolves went into retirement in 2018; their different characters have continued to give me inspiration. And I didn't make up the idea of Darkfur digging a spare den, she-wolves have been seen to do this in the wild.

I got the idea for Wolf's sore tail by chance, from my neighbours in Wimbledon. One evening I noticed that their beautiful black labrador, Iona, was looking miserable and couldn't move her tail. Until then I'd never heard of acute caudal myopathy, otherwise known as 'swimmer's tail'. So thank you, Iona – and thanks, too, to my delightful neighbours Dr Marta and Professor Sir Robin Murray, for telling me all about poor Iona's condition – which happily wore off after a few days, as did Wolf's.

Concerning the clans in *Wolfbane*, the inexhaustible inventiveness and creativity of hunter-gatherer cultures worldwide has continued to inspire me. The Kelps' flattened heads derive from the Kwakwaka'wakw (formerly Kwakiutl) and Coast Salish people. Many First Nations of the Pacific Northwest traditionally smeared their skin with a mix of red ochre, spruce pitch and fat, to protect against sun, wind and insects. The Kelps' habit of wearing bits of their dead crops up in many Pacific and South American peoples – as does preserving their dead in mummified or smoked form.

The Kelps' underground shelters are based on those of the Unangax and Alutiq people of the Aleutian and Pribilof Islands. Their belief that wolves and killer whales are the same spirit in two different bodies derives particularly from the Haida and Yupik. And the Coast Salish people used to train their much-respected dogs to chase deer out of the Forest, which some Pacific Northwest peoples traditionally believed was the haunt of demons and ghosts.

Kujai's canoe is similar in design and method of construction to those of the Haida and Makah people.

His spear, with its detachable head, and Fin-Kedinn's net-making gear, also derive from the Pacific Northwest. I got the idea for Naiginn's skis from the Chukchi of eastern Siberia, who traditionally used them for getting about the tundra. Naiginn's use of wolfbane, or aconite, is based on the hunting techniques of the Inuit, the Sugpiaq of Alaska and the Ainu of Japan.

It might strike you as impossible to make a horn by winding a long strip of birch bark and glueing it with pine tar, but I've seen such horns and I've heard one blown. On my first-ever research trip for *Wolf Brother* in 2003, while we were camping in the Finnish forest, our guide brought out a splendidly curved birch-bark horn and blew it. It sounded hauntingly evocative in the dark autumnal forest.

Finally, I've based Fin-Kedinn's funeral rites on the core beliefs of hunter-gatherers the world over. However I allowed the Raven Leader to get around the traditional prohibition against keeping mementoes of the dead, because I knew that, being Fin-Kedinn, he would find a way to comfort Torak, Renn and Dark – without breaking clan law.

Now I need to thank some people. First the crews and guides of *Island Roamer*, on which I explored Haida Gwaii; *Wilderness Adventurer*, for my trip to Alaska's Inside Passage and Glacier Bay National Park; and *MS Spitsbergen* of the

Hurtigruten Line, for the voyage from Kirkenes to Bergen. As before, particular thanks go to Jonathan Wright of Clearwell Caves: not only for showing me round the caves, but for taking me to see the Scowles, which helped inspire an episode in *Wolfbane*.

Throughout the series, Geoff Taylor's gorgeous chapter illustrations and endpaper maps have contributed enormously to evoking Torak's world; and for *Wolfbane* he has outdone himself with additional, magical double page spreads. I am so grateful to Geoff for his endless care, and his patience with my nit-picking. My gratitude, too, to John Fordham for his stunning designs for the original covers for the first six books, and for these last three volumes. I love them all, and fans do too.

I also want to thank the enthusiastic staff of my publishers, Head of Zeus, for their determination and hard work in bringing out *Wolfbane, Skin Taker* and *Viper's Daughter* in the teeth of the pandemic; and my particular thanks to the design team – Jessie Price, Ben Prior and Clémence Jacquinet – for turning *Wolfbane* into such a splendid volume.

I need to say very special thanks to Ian McKellen, who over the years has made time to record the audiobook of every story in the series. I've been present on every day of every recording, ostensibly to lend support and help with pronunciation and other queries, but really to marvel at Ian's ability to bring the stories to life. Watching him become Wolf, give voice to the human characters, and evoke demons, the Hidden People or the Sea Mother, has often sent shivers down my spine. He is a twenty-first century Mage.

Finally, I would like to thank the two people who made this series happen. First, my wonderful agent Peter Cox. It would never have occurred to me even to re-read my unpublished twenty-three-year-old story about a boy and a wolf if Peter hadn't encouraged me to think about writing different kinds of books. His overwhelmingly positive response when I first broached the idea of *Wolf Brother* encouraged me to believe in it, and since then he has given me and the books unflagging enthusiasm and support. I can't thank him enough.

Lastly, my thanks to Fiona Kennedy, my publisher and editor without peer. Fiona has lived and breathed Torak's world since *Wolf Brother*. I would not and could not have envisaged writing these three last sequels if I hadn't known that Fiona would be at the helm to steer them safely to port. I will always be grateful for her patience, her unflagging attention to detail, and her dauntless championing of my stories.

Michelle Paver,
London 2022

michellepaver.com
wolfbrother.com

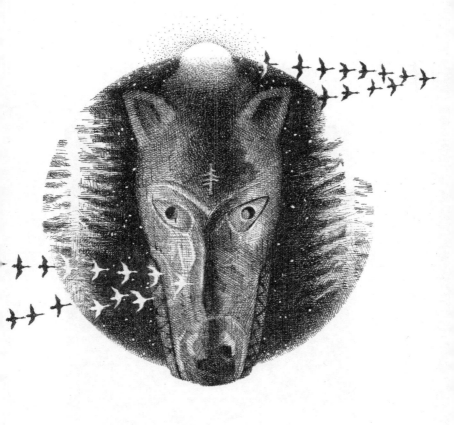

You can enjoy all
nine books in audio,
read by Sir Ian McKellen

A
LEGEND
FOR ALL
TIME

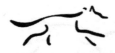

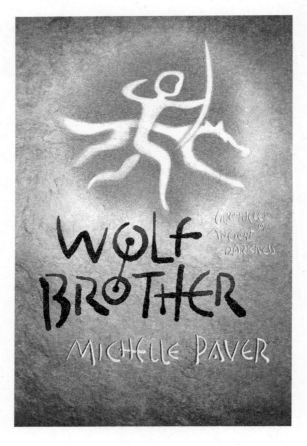

Torak finds himself alone in the Forest,
when his father is killed by a demon-haunted bear.

In his attempt to vanquish the bear, Torak makes
two friends who will change his life: Renn, the girl from
the Raven Clan, and Wolf, the orphaned wolf cub who
will soon become Torak's beloved pack-brother.

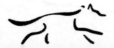

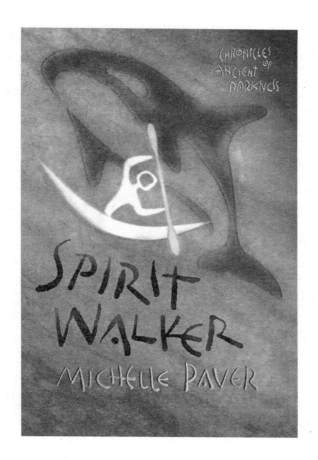

A horrible sickness attacks the clans,
and Torak has to find the cure.

His search takes him across the Sea to the
islands of the Seal Clan, where he encounters
demons and killer whales, and gets closer to
uncovering the truth behind his father's death,
as well as learning of his own undreamed-of-powers.

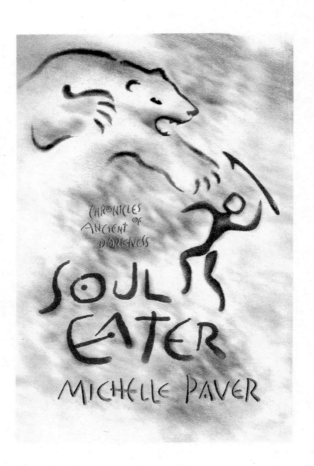

CHRONICLES OF ANCIENT DARKNESS

SOUL EATER

MICHELLE PAVER

Wolf is taken by the enemy.

To rescue him, Torak and Renn must journey
to the Far North in the depths of winter, where
they brave blizzards and ice bears, and venture into
the very stronghold of the Soul-Eaters.

Torak is alone and on the run.

Cast out of the clans, he hides out in the haunted
reedbeds of Lake Axehead, separated from Renn,
and even from Wolf.

CHRONICLES OF ANCIENT DARKNESS

OATH BREAKER

MICHELLE PAVER

One of Torak's closest friends is killed, and he tracks the murderer into the mysterious heart of the Deep Forest.

Here the clans are at war, and punish any outsider venturing in. In the Deep Forest, Torak learns more about his mother, and about just why he is the spirit walker.

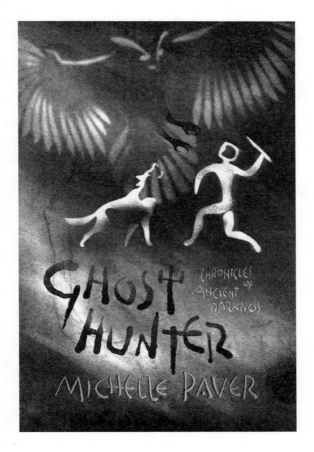

GHOST HUNTER

CHRONICLES OF ANCIENT DARKNESS

MICHELLE PAVER

Winter is coming and Souls' Night draws near.
Torak's quest leads to the high mountains, where
he must battle against the most fearsome of all
Soul-Eaters, Eostra the Eagle Owl Mage,
who seeks to rule both the living and the dead.

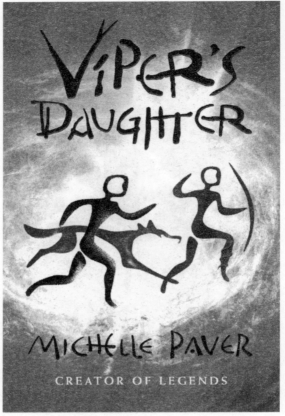

For two summers Torak, Renn and Wolf have
been living in the Forest. But their happiness is
shattered when Renn realizes Torak is in danger
– and she's the threat.

When Renn mysteriously disappears,
Torak and Wolf brave the Far North to find her.
Their quest leads them to the Edge of the World.

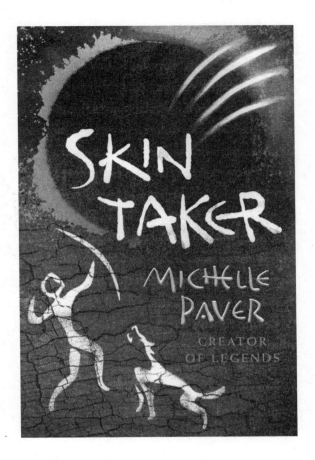

In the Dark Time of midwinter, disaster strikes
the Forest. Chaos rules. Only demons thrive.

With their world in turmoil, Torak, Renn and
Wolf are tested as never before. Torak must risk
his sanity, his life and even his souls to save
everything he loves.